The Mirror
and the Mountain

'I loved reading *The Mirror and the Mountain*.
I can honestly say that from the first page to the last
I was enthralled – from a magical kingdom
to a magical book."

– **Rob Parsons** (OBE), founder of Care for
the Family

"Opening up *The Mirror and the Mountain*
brought back the warm, fuzzy feelings of reading
The Famous Five and *The Secret Seven*. But as the story
went on, and the message behind Luke's storytelling
became clear, the warm fuzziness turned to joy
and surprise."

– **Jamie Cutteridge**, youth discipleship specialist at
The Salvation Army

"Luke has succeeded in creating a world of
rich imagery and powerful symbolism that could
help the whole family explore who Jesus is and
what he is like."

– **Gemma Willis**, Scripture Union content innovator
and author of the *Diary of a Disciple series*

"The stories that fill our worlds as kids
have the power to shape our entire lives. I think
every child should read this book, mainly because
they will love it but also because they'll be taking
something powerful into their souls that will
serve them well."

– **Rachel Gardner,** director of National Work at
Youthscape, co-founder of Romance Academy and
president of Girls' Brigade England and Wales

THE MIRROR AND THE MOUNTAIN

AN ADVENTURE IN PRESADIA

LUKE AYLEN

LION FICTION

Published by
Lion Hudson Limited
Wilkinson House, Jordan Hill Business Park,
Banbury Road, Oxford OX2 8DR, England
www.lionhudson.com

ISBN 978 1 78264 350 0
eISBN 978 1 78264 351 7

First edition published by Monarch Books, 2018

Text acknowledgments
Scripture quotations taken from the Holy Bible, New International Version,
copyright © 1973, 1978, 1984 International Bible Society. Used by permission
of Hodder & Stoughton, a member of the Hodder Headline Group. All rights
reserved. 'NIV' is a trademark of International Bible Society. UK trademark
number 1448790.

Cover image acknowledgments
Mirror © YaroslavGerzhedovich/iStockPhoto.com
Eye © Refluo/Shutterstock

A catalogue record for this book is available from the British Library

Printed and bound in the UK, January 2021, LH26

CONTENTS

Foreword		7
1	The Secret Passage	11
2	True Reflections	15
3	Gone	21
4	The Princess	24
5	Escape	31
6	The Long-Lost King	37
7	The Scavengers	43
8	Val-Chasar	49
9	The Dwarf Lord	55
10	The Dwarf's Deeds	61
11	Khoree's Lair	69
12	A Dragon's Riddle	74
13	The Dragon's Secret	79
14	The Tongue-Tamer	87
15	The Silver Wood	93
16	The Elfish Queen	101
17	Kidnap	105
18	The Quest to Find the King	110
19	Mount Necros	117
20	Khoree's Breath	121
21	The Chasm	127
22	The Dwarf's Treasure	134
23	The Crownless Queen	140
24	Mirror Mountain	144
25	Presadia Fallen	149

26 The King   154
27 The New Kingdom   160

Chapter Discussion Questions   168
The Mirror and the Mountain and James   173

FOREWORD

So what's a story for?

It's for enjoying, for a start. For laughter. For excitement. For adventure. For surprise. *The Mirror and the Mountain* has all of these in spades. And a boy and a girl to journey with – into a fantasy world populated by quirky and colourful characters.

But a story is also for discovering. Discovering something about the world, and others, and ourselves. *The Mirror and the Mountain* does that, too. It was originally written to support the teaching at a Christian conference called Spring Harvest, and specifically to help families understand the book of James in the Bible. And so it is also for discovering something about God.

In many ways, the story is a mirror itself, inviting readers to look at themselves, to see which characters they most resemble, and to discover the ways in which God might transform them, as the characters in the story are transformed.

It is not, however, "preachy" or "teachy" in a clumsy sort of way. What lessons or insights there are arise naturally from the struggles faced by the characters. In fact, one of the most admirable features of the book is that someone with no Christian background or interest could read it and enjoy it and be drawn into the story and inspired by those characters. Luke has very skilfully and sensitively woven the teaching of James into the narrative by doing what a good storyteller does – keeping the focus, first of all, on the story.

So if you are a Christian parent or children's worker or primary school teacher who would like to use the story to help your children understand the wisdom of James there is a section that helps you do this at the back of the book. There are also questions for each chapter at the end of the book to help you unpack the themes and lessons from a more neutral point of view if you still want to talk about what you are reading at school, home, or in a book club. And if not, just enjoy the story, because there is plenty to enjoy!

And that's the final thing a story is for. Sharing.

When my own children were growing up, we loved reading stories at dinner time, chapter by chapter. It brought us in contact with some wonderful tales, but it also brought us together. That's what a shared story does. It gives us the chance to journey together, at the time, but also provides a shared set of references and memories that last a lifetime. So the very best thing you can do with *The Mirror and the Mountain* is to share it. Read it with your children. Then laugh together, for there is a lot to laugh about. Worry together, for you never know what might happen to your favourite character. And wonder together at the way impossible odds are overcome by something impossibly better.

Look in the mirror. Climb the mountain. Be challenged, amazed, and changed.

Because that's what a story is for.

Bob Hartman, *author and performance storyteller, November 2017*

For Elijah, Jonah, Lucy, Ava, Summer, and Cub

Persevere from birth to grave,
For you are counted with the brave.

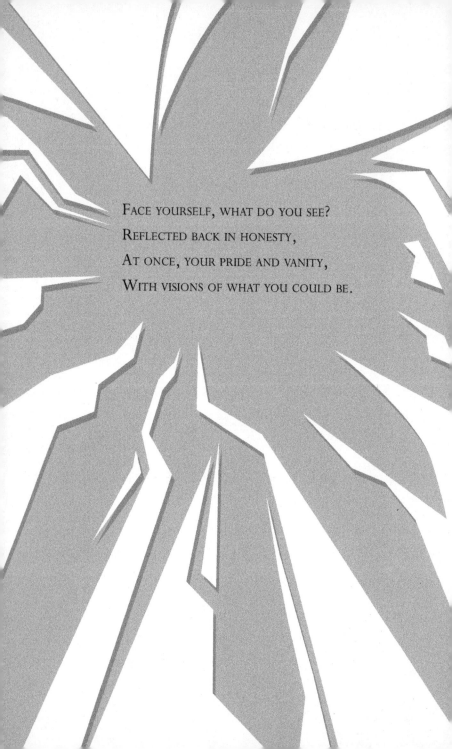

Face yourself, what do you see?
Reflected back in honesty,
At once, your pride and vanity,
With visions of what you could be.

1

THE SECRET PASSAGE

Jonah was running as fast as he could. His breath felt like fire as he gasped for air but he knew he couldn't stop – not unless he wanted to get caught.

He dodged between the towering grave stones that stuck up like crooked teeth from the rough unmown grass. He was nearing the familiar old church and knew a good hiding place. Without slowing, Jonah reached the wall of the church and slid across the damp grass into the shelter of a tiny doorway, about half his height. It was even shorter than he was and had a tiny porch. The perfect hiding place.

He leaned back against the door, panting. Peeking out, there was no one in sight. The graveyard was still. Jonah watched anxiously for anyone moving between the weathered stones. After a minute or so, he relaxed. He had lost his pursuer.

A smile broke across his face. No one could beat him when he was running. He was the fastest in his class. He leaned forward to sneak another glance out of his hidey-hole.

"Got you!" a voice shouted as the silhouette of a person stepped into the doorway.

Jonah jumped. He fell against the tiny door. It burst open. With an unexpected backward roll, he cartwheeled down some stairs into dusty darkness.

"Jonah!" the outline in the doorway cried out. "Are you OK?"

Jonah sat up and rubbed his bruised back. Enough light trickled down the steps for him to see that he had grazed his arm and that his slide into the doorway had left big grass stains on his jeans. His mum wouldn't be happy!

"Summer! You made me jump! How did you find me?" He tried to sound brave but his arm was stinging badly.

"Are you OK? Did you hurt yourself? Shall I go and get someone?"

Jonah could feel tears in the corners of his eyes but blinked them away.

"I'm OK," he managed. "You didn't tell me how you found me."

"You've hidden here loads of times, Jonah! When you ran in this direction, I knew you would come here." She sounded smug now that she was no longer worried about him. "What's down there? I've always wanted to know what was behind that door! It's so small, I'm surprised you fit through!" She was still peering down.

Jonah's eyes were adjusting to the dark and he could just make out her scrunched-up face as she squinted into the gloom. He peered around, repositioning himself onto his knees. He started to stand but bumped his head before he could get right up. Shuffling awkwardly, he tried to make sense of where he was.

By reaching out with his hands and straining his eyes, he could just about make out the walls of a little passageway stretching off into the darkness underneath the church.

"I think it's a secret tunnel!"

"Really?" Summer stooped to crawl through the little doorway and down the small flight of stairs that had given Jonah his bruises. As she felt her way, more light shone down. Jonah could see the huge stones that made up the walls and the dusty floor he kneeled on. The tunnel disappeared into blackness only a couple of metres further on behind thin curtains of spiderwebs.

"I can't see where it goes. I think we should go back. It might be dangerous." Jonah tried to sound sensible so Summer wouldn't realize how nervous he felt. It wasn't that he was scared of the dark – he was eleven years old, after all. It wasn't even that he was scared of spiders. But even an eleven-year-old can feel nervous about darkness *and* spiders!

"We can't go back yet! We need to explore first. Otherwise the grown-ups will lock the door and we will never know what's down here."

Summer had reached him and was trying to peep past.

It was true. If their parents knew they had found a secret tunnel under the church, they would definitely come and make sure it was locked up again.

"Maybe we can just look to the end of the tunnel…" Jonah mumbled, reluctantly dropping onto his hands and knees and shuffling deeper into the small space. Now they were down here, it couldn't do any harm to explore a few metres further. Also, he wasn't looking forward to his mum seeing the state of his jeans and his grazed arm.

The tunnel went on further than Jonah had thought. They must have crawled the whole length of the old village church, surely. Every now and again they would stop to listen in case they could hear the grown-ups in the church above drinking their tea and chatting, but the thick stones were silent. They might have been a mile underground; the silence was that complete.

It was so dark that Jonah only realized the tunnel had ended when he bumped his head.

"Ouch!"

"What is it?"

"Ouch!" Jonah repeated as Summer pushed into him, causing him to bump his head a second time. "Stop pushing me. I've reached the end."

"What's there?" She was still trying to squeeze around him.

Jonah fumbled blindly, feeling for the walls. In front and to one side of him was smooth, cold stone. But on his other side, he could feel a narrow set of steps rising beyond his reach.

"I think there is a way upstairs. It probably comes out in the church somewhere," he told Summer.

Carefully, he felt his way up. The ceiling opened out so that they could stand up straight as they started to climb. The steps were uneven and so steep and narrow it was almost like climbing a ladder, with the walls brushing them on either side. By the time they reached a corner, they were both feeling hot and achy.

"My legs are burning!" Jonah complained as they paused for a moment to catch their breath.

"Let's go on," Summer urged him after a minute or so.

"I'm not sure we should. Maybe we should go back. Our parents will probably be looking for us by now."

Jonah was the older by three months and knew he should be the responsible one.

"We can't turn back now! We might be right near the end," protested Summer. "What if there is treasure or something up here? Anyway, I think we are in the walls of the church. We've climbed quite a lot of steps – I want to know where they go. We aren't doing anything wrong. We haven't even left the church, after all."

With that, Summer squeezed past him. Jonah sensed a moment of panic when he heard her footsteps continuing up and away from him. He definitely didn't want to be left alone here in the dark. Chewing his lip, he hurried after her.

2

TRUE REFLECTIONS

Summer continued up the stairs despite the ache in her legs. She was feeling more confident at moving in the dark and could hear the comforting sound of Jonah a few steps below, grunting and scuffing his shoes on the uneven ground.

She hadn't wanted Jonah to think she was more afraid than he was, but still – it was good to know he was just behind her.

He was a noisy climber. He was always clumsier than she was. She was smaller and could often squeeze into places that Jonah didn't fit, and she didn't bump into everything like he did.

It came as a big surprise, therefore, when suddenly she banged her head hard against the ceiling. Stunned, she fell backwards, crashing into Jonah. For a moment Summer's heart skipped a beat as she thought of the long climb and what it would be like to tumble down and down in the darkness where no one would ever find them.

"Summer! Be careful – you almost made me fall backwards."

"I'm sorry. The stairs have ended and I hit my head!"

"They can't just end. Why would someone go to the effort of building stairs that go nowhere, silly?"

He pushed his way past her. She could hear his hands groping about in the dark.

"I don't know! Don't call me silly," she snapped. Maybe they *should* go back. Her head was aching and she was tired of this darkness and the cool damp silence of the hidden staircase. As secret tunnels went, it was exciting, but it was also a lot more unpleasant than she had expected.

"The roof here is made of wood, not stone," Jonah told her.

Summer heard more scratching and fumbling. She rubbed her head, probing for a bump and wondering if it was bleeding. Maybe she would pass out and get trapped here. She felt her confidence melting away, replaced by fear.

"Maybe you were right. Maybe we should go back," she said, hoping Jonah wouldn't hear how frightened she had started to feel.

"Don't be a scaredy-cat! You were the one who said we had to find the end. I think it's a trapdoor. Come and help me push."

The discovery of a trapdoor made her forget her sore head instantly. She wriggled her way up, grateful to feel Jonah's solid warmth as she stretched her arms to help push at the wooden panels above.

"I'll count to three," said Jonah. "One. Two. Three!"

The wood was heavy but it shifted as they pushed.

A slight crack appeared.

What they could see was not quite light – more a lighter shade of darkness – but still a huge relief to Summer, who was growing tired of the absolute blackness.

The heavy trapdoor thunked back into place again and the sliver of less-than-darkness disappeared.

"Come on! Again. And keep pushing this time." Jonah sounded excited now as he gave the order.

"One. Two. Eughhhhh…"

Jonah's "three" was lost in a groan of effort. Summer gritted her teeth and pushed with all her strength. The trapdoor lifted a few centimetres but no further. Both kept straining – and suddenly it gave. With the shriek of rusty hinges, the trapdoor swung upward and open, and Summer could see Jonah's outline in the grey light above.

He clambered up the final few steps and into the room. Summer followed and looked around.

The room they had entered was small and square. Light filtered down in one corner from a hole in the ceiling in one corner where some steep steps – almost a ladder – dropped down. A dozen or so slender poles ran from floor to ceiling, seeming to sway slightly. Summer wondered if she was dizzy from her bumped head but then realized these were ropes, dangling through holes in the ceiling above and continuing downward through holes in the floor. She tried to squint down the holes in the floor but the ropes fitted too snugly and the floorboards were too thick.

"Woah!" Jonah exclaimed, all traces of his earlier fear gone. "I think we are in the church tower. They use these ropes downstairs to ring the bells. Come on – I bet you that ladder leads up to the actual bells."

He scrambled up the ladder and disappeared through the hole above. Summer, hurrying to follow, pulled up short and jumped violently. Out of the corner of her eye, she caught a glimpse of something moving in the gloom. She spun and froze, her heart thudding so hard it hurt.

The shadowy person froze too.

She could just make out a silhouette, hidden in the darkness.

Relief and embarrassment at her own foolishness flooded through her. She was looking at a reflection of herself in a very old mirror. It was twice her height and as wide as a doorway. She moved closer, marvelling at the beautiful frame.

It was hard to make out the details in the murky light, but she could see things carved into the wood. There were mountains and faces, strange creatures and dragons. Even in the darkness where everything else seemed grey, the wonderful carvings almost glittered with vibrant colour. Summer could just make out elegant lettering threading its way through the designs. Running her fingers gently over the engravings, she whispered the words:

Face yourself, what do you see?
Reflected back in honesty,
At once, your pride and vanity,
With visions of what you could be.

She wasn't sure what "vanity" meant but the words sounded important and very wise. She gazed at her reflection in the mirror, looking herself up and down. She was dusty from her adventure through the tunnel. She smiled at how brave and adventurous she looked.

The reflection in the mirror seemed brighter than the room around her.

It flickered.

It seemed as if she saw a flash of herself somewhere else; it was the briefest of glimpses, but she remembered the moment. That day in the playground when she teased the new girl. She hadn't meant to be mean; she had just been going along with what everyone else was doing. The image vanished but Summer was ashamed of the memory.

She blinked. Her imagination was running away with her. *Too long in the dark*, she thought to herself.

The mirror flickered.

Her elder sister was there, being told off for something Summer had done. Summer was smirking behind her mum's back.

The mirror flickered.

She was crying in her bedroom, too terrified to sleep.

The mirror flickered.

One after the other, reflections flashed across the mirror. Some showed her at the times she had been bad or dishonest. Others showed her times when she had been afraid or sad or jealous. The images blurred as tears began to slide down her dusty face. The mirror was showing sides of herself she never wanted others to see – the secrets she hid and the unflattering and unkind thoughts she had.

Not all the moments were bad. Some showed incidents she was proud of and times she had been good, done kind things, or helped someone else. But as each scene flashed by, the mirror reflected back more than just her image; it reflected *her*. What she was like inside as well as out. It was as if she looked *into* the reflection rather than at it.

As the flickering slowed and stopped, Summer continued to stare. All she could see now was her normal reflection – and yet it was different. Something was missing. For a moment, it was as though she were an unfinished painting, almost complete but not quite. Gradually – was this just her imagination? – her reflection was transforming. Nothing changed about her appearance but she became more vivid, more real. She was seeing herself completed, the finished person she was meant to be.

Suddenly the mirror changed.

Her image was gone. Instead there was just the murky darkness of the room. At least, that was what she thought at first. But she could see the dim outlines of furniture. The bell ropes were gone and there was light beading through the cracks of a door in the corner. She looked behind her to make sure her eyes were not tricking her. The mirror wasn't reflecting the church tower. It was showing another room, one of a similar size but definitely different.

She moved closer to the mirror and more of the space beyond became visible, as though the mirror had become a window. The room beyond looked as though it was in a stately home or very posh house. Wanting to see more, Summer pressed closer to the glass.

Her feet knocked against the bottom of the mirror.

In terrible slow motion, the towering mirror began to fall toward her. As it gained speed, Summer froze with fear.

Jerking back to her senses, she tried to jump out of the way but it was too late. She screamed as the mirror glass hit her.

3

GONE

Jonah pulled himself through the hole at the top of the ladder and looked around.

The light was brighter up here. Behind large shutters – set in tall arches – were strips of sky. Around him, from dark wooden beams that were broader than he was, hung four enormous church bells.

"Woah!" Jonah exclaimed to himself as he wove his way between the ropes that dropped from the big metal levers attached to each bell through the floor to the room below.

Below him, a panicked scream, cut off by a loud bang, made him start.

"Summer!" he shouted, scrambling back to the hole that led downstairs. Had Summer fallen back through the trapdoor and caused it to slam shut on her?

He practically fell down the ladder, missing a few rungs in his rush and landing with a bump in the room below.

"Summer? What happened?"

He squinted, his eyes readjusting to the darkness of the room. Impatiently, he fumbled his way back across it, searching for the trapdoor that led to the hidden stairs.

"Have you fallen down? I'm coming. Wait, I'll open the trapdoor. Are you hurt?"

There was no reply. Jonah, panicking, reached the trapdoor and almost fell through the open hole in the floor. He caught himself and felt around. It was still open – just as they had left it.

Peering down the passage, he frowned.

"Summer? Where are you? Are you down there?"

No response.

Summer was gone.

Carefully, worried he might stumble into whatever had caused that bang and made Summer scream, he shuffled his way around the room. With his night vision returning, he searched desperately around for any clue.

He stubbed his toe.

"Ouch!"

Crouching down, he examined what had tripped him. It appeared to be the back of a big painting or picture frame. He hadn't noticed it earlier. It was solid-looking and certainly could have caused the bang.

The frame vibrated against his hands. He jerked back as if it had burned him. The floor wasn't moving but he was sure he could hear a rattling sound. Resting his hands against the frame again, he felt the vibrations get stronger. Summer had to be under there! Maybe there was another trapdoor, or maybe she had fallen through the floor! The church was very old, after all, and this room didn't look as if it was ever used.

"Summer! Summer! Can you hear me? Hold on, I'll get you out!"

Squeezing his fingers under the edge of the fallen frame, he heaved up with all his strength. It was heavy and solid but he could just lift it on his own. As he did, light spilled out from underneath. He bent down to look, straining his muscles to hold it in place.

He dropped the frame in shock, causing another loud bang. There wasn't another trapdoor, or even a hole in the floor – just plain old floorboards. Inside the frame, however, Jonah had glimpsed a room, much the same size as this one, but with an open door leading outside.

He blinked, sure he must be seeing things, but there was a purple rectangle burned into his vision from the brightness of the door. He blinked again, waiting for it to fade, breathing heavily.

There couldn't be another room inside the frame: it was impossible. He could see the back of the frame. He could feel it. But his eyes hadn't lied. There was a room through the frame. He knew it certainly and completely. He also knew without a doubt that Summer had gone through. He didn't know why, but he was sure he had to follow.

He sat down on the floor. Once more he pulled up the frame, awkwardly lifting it as much as he could while lying on his back.

Slowly, inch by inch, he shuffled underneath and through.

4

THE PRINCESS

The smash of glass she had dreaded never came. Instead, there was a loud bang as the mirror frame landed squarely on the floor.

Summer peered around her, wondering what had happened. She was huddled in the middle of the empty frame.

No, not an empty frame. She was standing on the back of the mirror. Straightening up, she looked around her. She was in the grand room she had seen beyond the mirror. Somehow the mirror had fallen right through her – or she through the mirror.

Very carefully she tiptoed off the back of the frame. The room was dark, but not as dark as the church tower. Light trickled in from around the door and the shuttered windows.

The furniture was big and ornate. Through the gloom, she could make out dramatic pictures of battles and forests on the walls. There was also noise. She could hear cheering, shouting, and a loud commotion somewhere outside. That definitely hadn't been there a moment ago.

Sudden panic seized her.

What had happened? Where was she? What if someone suddenly came in and found her here, or the owner of the mirror had heard it falling over?

A crash and rumble shook the room.

This adventure was becoming scary. Scrambling around under the church had been fun, but now it was all starting to feel weird and unfamiliar. She needed to go back. Where was Jonah? She wanted to be with him again.

Crouching down, she dug her fingers under the mirror frame and pulled with all her might. It was so heavy! She managed to lift it a couple of centimetres before dropping it.

The mirror rattled against the floorboards.

Swallowing the panic that threatened to make her cry, she tried again. She wasn't strong enough.

After a third try, she gave up.

Be sensible, she told herself. There had to be another way back. She looked around the room searching for something – anything! – to help.

There was a table, covered with goblets and gleaming silverware, but nothing that could help her. A flash of light caught her eye and she saw a ring with a lovely blue gemstone. For an instant, its captivating beauty made her forget her fear. *It wouldn't hurt just to try it on, would it – just to see what it would look like?*

She picked it up and slipped it on. It was a tight fit, but still, it looked wonderful on her slender finger, as if it had been crafted just for her. She held out her hand to admire how she looked and, for a moment, felt like royalty.

Another crash broke her daydream, the vibrations so strong she could feel them through the floor. She stopped to listen. Out of the general hullabaloo and distant shouting, she could make out some more distinct voices, becoming clearer, coming nearer to the door of her room.

Maybe the ring had made her feel braver, but Summer suddenly made up her mind. She was going to need help if she was going to get back to Jonah.

Heaving the huge latch, she pulled the door open – and stared in astonishment.

In front of her stretched a walkway, high atop the ramparts of a castle, zigzagging out of sight, making it impossible for her to see far along the top of the wall. On one side rose battlements, and on the other was a dizzying drop to a courtyard full of mismatched buildings where people ran around like ants. The room behind her was part of a tall square tower in the corner of the castle, soaring high into the stormy clouds overhead. There was a heavy warm mist, which added a yellowy haziness to the scene.

She hastily moved back from the edge that dropped away. It made her stomach lurch. Instead, she stood on tiptoe to peek out between the defences. The view on this side was no less spectacular, and a good deal more frightening.

A humid gust of wind momentarily parted the mist, revealing a scene that took her breath away.

Below her was a vast, sweeping landscape, a patchwork of fields and woods. A river meandered lazily back and forth. Further in the distance, the fields became meadows, before turning into forests, carpeting soft hills that grew bigger and bigger until they blended into the vague silhouettes of towering mountains, just visible on the horizon.

It was arranged like a beautiful painting, and would have been a stunning view if not for the oppressive fog. It smothered the scenery like a damp blanket, wafting in great clouds, dulling the light and sucking colour from what should have been a vivid landscape. In places the fog was so thick that it caused great opaque tendrils like thick feathery fingers. It gave Summer the impression of an enormous warped hand crushing the countryside in its evil grip.

The fields near the castle had turned to mud and were scattered with blackened rubble. They were crawling with many more people than the courtyard on her other side was.

Large spidery contraptions, complex wooden machines loaded with chunks of broken masonry, lumbered toward the castle. Some looked like pictures of catapults she had seen, while others were unfamiliar, tall tepee-like structures with a massive sling between them. As she stared, the arm of one gigantic catapult swung upward, hurling a chunk of rock in her direction. Almost in slow motion, it smashed into another tower, the exact likeness of the one behind her, in the next corner of the castle. It was accompanied by a deafening crash, and the castle shook again with the impact. Bricks and wood exploded out from the damaged wall.

She had seen pictures of castles under siege in school. Never had she dreamed she would find herself in the middle of such an alarming affair. There was an army outside, trying to get in, and it looked as if they were doing a good job. The pictures in school hadn't made it look so dangerous and messy, though. What was she to do? A castle siege was no place for an eleven-year-old girl!

The sound of approaching voices made her turn back to the walkway. She couldn't see anyone around the twists and turns, but they were definitely coming closer.

"Tally-ho! Make way there!"

"Great Potash's beard, this is a dangerous place!"

Another lump of rock hit the castle and shook the whole building.

"I say! That was a close one! Out of my way, Antimony!"

She ran in the direction of the voices, no longer thinking of the drop down to the courtyard on her left. Each turn of the zigzagging walkway brought another stretch into view and the voices closer.

"I think it's time to make a speedy exit."

"I quite agree. Get a move on, Clay. We've done our bit. We've sold all our stock. I'd rather not get buried under a fallen castle. Why Lord Raven insisted on staying on the walls this long, I'll never know. It would have been much safer to do business in the courtyard."

Summer turned another corner and ran face first into a grown man. Well, kind of grown. In truth, he hadn't grown very far. He was almost as short as she was.

She jumped and the little man, equally surprised, gave out a high-pitched scream, so at odds with his gruff, bearded appearance that it distracted Summer from how strange he looked to her.

He slid to a halt and his four companions bumped into him, domino-fashion.

There was a moment of awkward silence.

"You're very small," Summer blurted out, without thinking.

"So are you!" replied the little man, sounding offended. "We're dwarfs. What's your excuse?"

They were all wearing armour. Summer couldn't help thinking it looked more decorative than useful. Each dwarf appeared to be trying to outdo the others with quiffs and engravings, and sparkling jewels embedded into the metalwork. Their faces were grimy, but rosy cheeks poked out from between bushy eyebrows and long, long beards. So long, in fact, that Summer had initially thought they were thick woolly scarves wrapped around their necks. A couple had them plaited; the others had gemstones and coloured thread woven into them. Summer was sure that if the beards had been unwound they would have been longer than the dwarfs were tall.

"I say, Clay, where are your manners?" A dwarf from the middle of the small group shouldered his way to the front. "This young lady must be the princess."

"The princess?" Clay looked her up and down doubtfully. "I didn't think this castle had a princess."

"Don't be silly. Every castle has a princess, you rock head!"

"Perhaps she's a handmaiden," a voice from the back piped up helpfully. Summer didn't think the speaker was a dwarf. Although he was dressed like the others, he towered above them, his spotty face sporting only a wispy attempt at a beard.

"No, no, no, Antimony. Everyone knows handmaidens have very big hands…"

Alarmed, Summer lifted her hands to check how large they were.

"And look! No handmaiden would wear a ring like that!"

Summer jerked back her hand to cover the ring. She had forgotten about it! Would she get into trouble for taking it? Maybe not, if they thought she was somebody as important as a princess. Most of the dwarfs were not looking convinced. She would need to convince them. She was wearing a dress, and for the first time, she felt grateful that her mum always made her wear one when they went to church. She smoothed it, brushing off some of the dust and cobwebs, and held herself up as straight as she could.

"I am indeed the princess," she said in her poshest voice. "I'm a princess visiting from… a far-off kingdom, so you must obey me. I need you to help me. There's a mirror in–"

"See, she's a princess!"

"I'm really not sure she–"

"Silence, Clay. You're interrupting the princess."

"But you interrupted her first!"

"I said silence!" The loud dwarf, who appeared to be in charge, bashed Clay's helmet with his armoured fist, making a sound like a dropped kitchen pan.

"Your highness," he said, bowing low. "I am Salt, your humble servant." He remained bent double, waiting. The other dwarfs shuffled awkwardly before bobbing small bows of varying enthusiasm.

"Pleased to meet you, Salt," replied Summer in her most ladylike voice. "My name is Princess Summer. Now about this mirror. It's–"

"I would, of course, consider it my duty to offer you my protection and assistance in saving you from this castle. I fear it will not stand much longer against this army, your highness. They have some of the finest siege weapons and catapults around."

"Only because they bought them from us!" Antimony, the tall one, chirped in proudly.

Summer tried again. "I don't want to leave the castle. I need to go back–"

"Nonsense, your highness. You are what we like to call a dandelion in distress."

"Isn't it a damsel?" Clay muttered.

Salt ignored him, continuing his heroic speech. "By my wife's beard, I swear I would never desert a lady in need. Come on, now – no time to dally. Antimony, help the young princess along, please."

The dwarfs bundled forward. Antimony looked momentarily confused as to how to "help her along", before shrugging and throwing Summer over his shoulder, ignoring her squeal of protest. She had no choice but to go with them.

5

ESCAPE

Jonah rolled. The heavy frame crashed back to the floor with the sound of shattering glass. Scrambling to his feet, he looked down at the mess. The frame lay face down but the back was gone. Shards of broken mirror were scattered over the floorboards. They glittered in the gloom.

Peering closer, Jonah thought each shard showed a slightly different reflection. He wouldn't have been able to explain it if he had tried, but it seemed as if each piece reflected a different side of him. All the images *looked* like him, but there was something deeper than what he saw with his eyes. It was as if he glimpsed a flash of the selfish part of him, a flicker of the fear he often felt, a glimmer of his desires, a snatch of his hopes.

So many reflections, and not all of them flattering. In fact, more than a few of them made him squirm.

The shards flickered again. The reflections changed. Instead of showing him what he was, they seemed now to show the kind of person he would prefer to be. Brave, generous, truthful, kind. The images were mesmerising... Oh, how he longed to be truly like that!

A deep boom jerked him back from his daydream, pounding his eardrums. The whole room shook, the mirror shards tinkling like wind chimes. He looked back but the mysterious images were gone, replaced by ordinary reflections in the hundreds of broken pieces. The memory remained, though – those images of him as he truly was, and those that showed what he could become. He would not forget.

Jonah looked around. This definitely wasn't the church tower. Light from an open door showed him a grand room, like something from a medieval castle, with ornate furniture fit for a king.

Summer was nowhere to be seen.

Jonah crossed to the open doorway and looked out, his mouth falling open as he stared at the scene in front of him. Dazed, he took a few steps along the top of an abandoned wall with a dizzying drop to one side and glimpses of fields, trees, and mountains on the other. A whistling sound behind him made him spin around in time to see a rock the size of his kitchen table smash into the room he had just left. Lumps of stone and clouds of dust exploded outwards and Jonah stumbled backwards in fear. The rock had ripped a hole larger than a car into the wall of the tower.

Jonah's hearing was strangely muffled. He had barely noticed the general hubbub and noise of battle until the crash had deafened him. Now all he could hear was a high-pitched ringing.

Clambering to his feet, he ran back to the doorway and peered into the mess beyond. The room was unrecognizable. A large section of the floor had fallen away and the gaping hole in the wall made it seem as if he was looking at an open doll's house. The furniture was smashed and there was no sign of the broken mirror.

"What are you doing? Get out!" A man's voice pierced its way through the ringing in Jonah's ears.

He looked behind him. There was a man on the walkway. He looked haggard and grimy, his hair slicked back with sweat. He wore armour made not from metal but from layers of worn leather that protected his chest, arms, and the tops of his legs. He was gesturing frantically. With a look of frustration, he started toward Jonah at a jog.

"We are abandoning the walls and retreating to the keep. I thought everyone had gone already. The enemy has broken through on the east side."

"My f-friend," Jonah stammered. "I need to find Summer..."

The man didn't hear.

"Come now. It's not safe here." He took Jonah by the collar. Jonah, confused and shaken, allowed himself to be dragged along the top of the wall. As the ringing in his ears decreased, his hearing returned and so did his wits. He regained his feet and began to run. The man didn't let go, though, forcing Jonah to keep up a fast pace. They reached a staircase and the man went down, two steps at a time.

Jonah was grateful for the man's grip, preventing him from tripping or falling. When they reached the courtyard, he let go, and Jonah stumbled to a halt. The man kept running.

"Wait! I need to find my friend Summer!"

The man slowed, and looked back at Jonah.

"All the soldiers are pulling back to the keep for the final defence–"

"She's not a soldier – she's my age," Jonah replied desperately.

The man paused, impatience battling concern on his face.

"What's she still doing here? There should be only soldiers left." He frowned. "They have opened the sally port at the back of the blacksmith's yard. A group of dwarfs snuck through to us with supplies, and the injured soldiers are escaping while they can. If there are any villagers or servants left, they'll be heading there too. The castle won't hold out much longer and it will be the last chance to get out." He pointed before turning and continuing his run to the keep.

Jonah ran to where the man had pointed. There were many

others running in different directions. Almost all were soldiers, like the one who had helped him.

Through an arch, Jonah continued across another courtyard, which was lined with straw-thatched buildings. One was on fire and a group of soldiers were passing buckets of water in a long chain to be thrown onto the flames.

Ahead of him, Jonah saw a woman dragging two children. For a moment, he wondered if one was Summer but then realized they were both small boys: grubby, and wearing loose, ill-fitting clothing.

He followed them, anyway, hoping they would lead him to the sally port, whatever that was. There were a few others who didn't look like soldiers running in the same direction.

The sally port, it turned out, was a small, ordinary-looking door, like a garden gate, in the wall of the castle. It was open. An exhausted soldier was beckoning the scared people through.

"Excuse me," Jonah shouted into the chaos, "have you seen a girl, about this tall, wearing a white dress?"

"What?" The man, trying to push Jonah through the door with the other fleeing people, looked distracted.

"My friend. A little girl in a white dress."

"Yes. I think so. A few minutes ago. With the weapon sellers."

"The weapon sellers?"

"Yes, the dwarfs. Now be gone with you. You're the last. Go, unless you want to pull back to the keep and fight."

Confused, but not wanting to miss his chance to leave, Jonah followed the worried, bustling crowd through the doorway.

The door opened onto some narrow steps that clung to a small cliff face with woodland at the bottom. There was no easy place for the enemy to attack this side and the chaos and noise dissipated as he left the busyness of the courtyard. The noises of battle were more distant and muffled as he hurried down the uneven stairs.

Very soon, Jonah caught up with the other people fleeing the castle. He hopped from foot to foot in frustration at how slowly they shuffled down the steps. He tried to peer around for any sign of the "weapon sellers". Had the man said they were dwarfs? Surely dwarfs were just made-up creatures, from stories. Then again, Jonah had thought a lot of things impossible before his tumble through the mirror. He wished he were taller and could see over the heads of the crowd.

"Excuse me." He tapped the shoulder of a woman in front of him. "Can you see any dwarfs ahead of us?"

She looked a similar age to his mum, and the worried expression she wore as she looked him up and down only deepened the resemblance. She wore a simple brown dress with a white apron, and Jonah wondered if she was a servant from the castle. The woman scanned the queue. "I can't see no dwarfs. But then they be little ones, so they could be among the others." She looked at him more closely. "What you be wantin' with folk like dwarfs?"

"My friend has gone. I think she's with the dwarfs. I need to find her."

"I'd be careful about goin' off with dwarfs. Seem like nice folk, but they be greedier than a dragon. They don't care who they stand on to get their shiny loot. What's your friend doing mixin' with them?"

"I don't know. I just need to find her."

"Well, you'll see them soon enough, I reckon. You know the saying, 'If there's money to be made, through dwarfs you must wade.' Silly old saying but it's truth, nonetheless. They love a good battle. I saw dwarfs 'ere earlier, looking to sell supplies to Lord Raven. Dreadful little creatures! There wouldn't be no battle if they hadn't sold those throwing machines to Lord Brookford. Sell swords to a pair of grumpy old men and they're sure to start a fight. I'd be gettin' as far away from here as you can, boy. 'Ere – you're young to be alone. Where are your folks?"

"They're not here. It's complicated but I have to find my friend and get back to them."

The shuffling mass had reached the bottom of the staircase and the crowd was dispersing in different directions. The woman made as if to follow the group in front of her, but paused, turning back to Jonah.

"It's not safe bein' alone out here. I don't know how long the castle will hold, but a battle's a battle. If you've got no folks, why don't you come with me?"

Jonah was tempted. He had never felt so alone – or so scared – in his life. But he couldn't just abandon Summer. He had to find her.

"I can't. But thank you."

She looked at him, long and hard. Then she nodded.

"So be it. Take care, boy. You've got the king's courage in you, that's for sure."

With that, she hurried after the others.

Jonah hesitated as he wondered what to do. There was no sign of the weapon-selling dwarfs. Well, first things first. He needed to get safely away from the castle before things got worse. He picked a direction at random and set off.

6

THE LONG-LOST KING

The journey from the castle had been a blur to Summer. The dwarfs had bundled her along, ignoring all her protests.

After coming down from the walls, they had rushed her through the castle and out of a small door. At the bottom of a set of steps were two unhappy dwarfs with a couple of empty carts and a small herd of ridiculous-looking long-haired ponies. Their silky coats hung almost to the ground, and they were topped with saddles that looked more like miniature thrones. The two dwarfs were unsuccessfully trying to calm the jittery animals by grooming them with pearl-handled brushes, but every crash from the castle siege brought with it the danger of a stampede and innumerable split ends.

It was on these strange ponies that they continued their journey. Summer had never ridden a pony before and it took three dwarfs to settle her into the saddle. Once mounted, to her surprise her carpet on legs seemed content to do its own thing and the cushioned, high-backed saddle was almost comfortable. She had no idea how her golden-haired pony could see anything from behind its curtain of a mane, but it trotted along merrily with the rest of the hairy herd without Summer needing to do much at all. By watching how the others used the reins, she managed to steer her animal.

The reins themselves appeared to be plaited from what Summer strongly suspected was dwarfish beard hair.

The other dwarfs politely ignored the laughable appearance of Antimony, the "tall dwarf", on his miniature animal. His feet dragged along the ground, and Summer wondered if he might have got along faster simply by walking.

After an initial descent into the misty valley, over which the castle stood watch, the journey was almost entirely uphill. To begin with, there were the woods that hugged the back edge of the castle, but soon these opened onto lush meadows, cloaked in ghostly clouds of ever-present fog. The meadows gently sloped up the valley edge, becoming distinct hills that led them higher and higher. The mountains loomed ever closer, and the patches of mist grew thicker. The dwarfs seemed to distrust the fog and steered around the densest areas. After they had been riding for a few hours, Summer turned back in her saddle to see how high they had climbed.

A cool breeze fluttered through her hair and opened up a brief window through the mist. The view behind was even more dramatic than that from the castle top. She could see the whole stretch of the fertile valley. Fields, villages, and pockets of woodland were like little islands in the fog. Towering over its domain was the once-proud castle. Even in its battered and damaged state, Summer could see it must have once been an incredibly beautiful structure. The drama of the scene centred around the castle. Great sections of the high wall had tumbled down or were smashed in. Soldiers were streaming in through a particularly large breach in the wall and the spindly, wooden siege equipment was finally still. A moment later and the scene was gone, instantly replaced by the clouded wall of yellowy haze.

Only two of the four towers remained standing. Summer wondered if her mirror room was in one of them, but the confusing rush from the castle meant she had lost all sense of direction. She prayed the mirror had survived. For all she knew, it could be the only way back, and she longed to get home as quickly as possible.

Salt interrupted her thoughts. "I realize you must feel great distress to have witnessed such a thing. A siege is no place for a young princess such as yourself. Not at all!"

Summer gave occasional nods and smiles to encourage Salt. He had kept up an endless flow of flowery words for the last few hours. Summer was grateful. With all she had been through – not to mention the need to keep up her pretence about being a princess – she barely knew what to say. He seemed quite content chatting away, and Summer only chipped in occasionally so as not to seem rude.

"Fires below! I don't know how Lord Raven could possibly neglect you so badly. I mean, I know he is under siege and all, but he really was being a terrible host, leaving you in that dangerous tower. A visiting princess, nonetheless!

"It's a pity that you had to visit Presadia at this time. Things are not like they used to be. Many, many years ago this kingdom was the fairest place there ever was. There weren't so many problems then. Of course, the wars have not been entirely bad for us. We've moved with the times – adapted – learned how to make the best of a bad situation. War can be quite profitable, really. We are the best engineers and weaponsmiths in the land, you know. If someone needs something, we can provide it. But it's said that when the king was here, there was never a single war – just think of that! Before my time, of course."

"Where did the king go?" Summer asked, to show that she was listening.

"Where exactly? I'm not sure. It was hundreds of years ago now. The king was fair and loved by the people – and Presadia thrived, with elves, dwarfs, humans, and all the other races working together. It was said that there was nowhere in all creation as beautiful."

"What happened?" asked Summer, genuinely interested now.

"The king was kind and generous, but alas, some of his servants were selfish. They wanted to control Presadia themselves and have all the wealth and glory. They plotted to overthrow the king. Legend has it that they rose up against him and exiled him from the kingdom."

"That's dreadful!"

Salt let out a big sigh.

"Yes. Yes, it is. Not long after the king was exiled, all the problems started. The wicked servants fought among themselves over who would have the most power. The elves tried to restore control and order – the king was betrothed to marry one, you know. Things didn't go to plan, however, and the elves – who are a stubborn bunch at the best of times – left the rest of the kingdom to its own devices. The king's betrothed became queen of the elves. No one sees much of them these days. Some of the rarer races have died off or fled Presadia entirely. The humans have been the worst. They started waging war with each other and doing terrible things. The beauty and brilliance of the kingdom began to fade, like tarnished silver in need of a good polish. It is but a shadow of what it used to be."

"That's so sad."

"It certainly is. And I don't think it's going to get any better. Even in the time since I was a babe playing around with my first axe, things have become worse. When I was young, I remember the summer days being long and filled with sunshine. The earth gave up jewels and precious metals by the bucketload. No longer. Even the weather seems to mourn the loss of the king. Now there are more storms than sunny days, and the sunlight is a rare and wonderful thing. Most of the time this horrible mist hangs around us. Even the land seems to be groaning. The grass withers, the trees are diseased, the streams that were once crystal clear are now thick and brown. We find only stone and dirt in the mines."

Summer looked around as he continued the sad story. She could see the truth of what he said. The countryside was still beautiful, but there was a sadness to it. Closer inspection showed that the green grass was patched with yellow and brown. The trees had leaves that were mottled with black marks. The air felt damp and tasted slightly rotten. The dwarfs kept a watch around them with an alertness that signalled danger could be around any corner.

"Many in Presadia suffer the coughing sickness. Even some dwarfs. It is sad, my lady, that you should see this kingdom so. But what is a kingdom without its king?" He sighed again.

"Anyhow, enough of this sadness! We make the best of things. We dwarfs have always prided ourselves on being able to bring the best out of any situation. A rotten tree can still feed the furnace, as my father used to say. And where there's war, there's money to be made.

"We dwarfs are true followers of the king. We faithfully wait for his return. Of that we are proud. But we have carved out a nice little kingdom of our own! You'll see it soon. The mighty chasm of Val-Chasar is a sight to behold. I am jealous of you. You get to experience it for the first time today. The jewel of the dwarfs is beyond anything you can imagine, my lady."

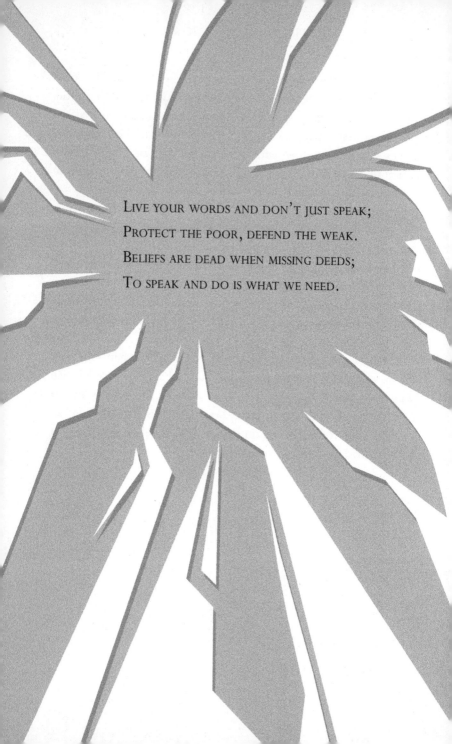

LIVE YOUR WORDS AND DON'T JUST SPEAK;
PROTECT THE POOR, DEFEND THE WEAK.
BELIEFS ARE DEAD WHEN MISSING DEEDS;
TO SPEAK AND DO IS WHAT WE NEED.

7

THE SCAVENGERS

Jonah's feet were aching. He had been walking for hours. He had lost count of the number of fields he had crossed when he came upon one that made him stop and stare. A battle had clearly happened here, and not too long ago. The field was scattered with broken catapults and random debris. Colourfully striped tents looked strangely out of place in the churned-up mud.

In the middle of the field was a large wooden wagon, piled high with glittering metal. Swords, shields, and other valuables were stacked neatly. Around the cart was a buzz of activity, in the middle of which was a group of children wearing big fur coats and metal hats.

His heart leaped within him when he realized they weren't coats and hats but beards and helmets. These were not children; they were the dwarfs!

Forgetting his achy feet, he started purposefully across the battlefield toward the wagon, looking hopefully for Summer. There were other, raggedly dressed people roaming the field, stooping over and poking among the debris left by the battle and occasionally picking things up to examine them. Jonah watched them for a moment wondering what they were up to. Most of the time they simply cast aside their finds, but occasionally someone would hurry toward the wagon carrying their salvage.

Jonah had to look down in order to pick his way through the mess. The ground was littered with all kinds of things: scraps of torn clothing, mud-covered breastplates, dented helmets, various weapons, broken wood, and items that must have been part of an army camp before the battle. It was all trodden down into the thick mud and, more than once, Jonah had to climb onto the debris to avoid sinking into the ravaged soil.

As he neared the wagon, a flash of brightness caught his attention. Leaning down, he brushed away a scrap of dirty fabric and pulled from the mud a wooden handle with golden engravings and sparkling jewels. It was larger than he had expected. As he pulled it out from the mud, he saw it was the length of his arm, solid and heavy. He stared in amazement.

It was a beautiful axe. Jonah could see the silver head under its coating of mud, with a long, curved blade and a purple jewel where it met the handle. It must have been worth a lot of money and have belonged to someone very important. He used his sleeve to try and clean away some of the mud and examined the golden engravings on the handle. Spiralling around the smooth polished wood was beautiful swirly writing:

> *Live your words and don't just speak;*
> *Protect the poor, defend the weak.*
> *Beliefs are dead when missing deeds;*
> *To speak and do is what we need.*

The sound of raised voices by the wagon dragged his attention away from the mysterious axe and reminded him of his mission. Gripping his prize in both hands, he continued on his way, keeping a careful watch for any more treasures. There was still no sign of Summer, but if these short people were indeed dwarfs, they might know where she was.

At the wagon, an argument was taking place. A ragged woman, desperation in her voice, was shouting, "You really can't be serious. This is worth a hundred times what you are offering!"

"Supply and demand, woman!" shouted back a grumpy dwarf. "We are up to our ears in swords. I don't see anyone else on this field buying them. A copper is fair money."

"Nonsense," scoffed the outspoken woman. "That won't buy me an apple! You'll make a fortune from this wagonload – and what have you given us in return?"

"You can't blame us for the way business works. That's my final offer. Take it or move on."

The woman scowled for a moment, then made as if to leave, before changing her mind and stepping up to tower over the dwarf.

"You make us slave away and don't give us enough to even feed ourselves. This whole battle was your fault anyway. You've been stirring up trouble between Lord Brookford and Lord Raven for years, just so you can make your money selling them both weapons. You've turned war into business and you are exploiting us all just to make yourself richer!"

The grumpy dwarf was red-faced, and spluttered as he tried to get a word in. The woman's righteous anger wouldn't be interrupted. A crowd was forming around the wagon. Jonah squeezed in; around him, other ragged men, women, and children were grumbling in agreement with the angry woman.

"You don't care that our homes were destroyed. You don't care that our families are gone. You don't even mind using our children to roam the battlefield for your loot. You get richer while we get poorer. Why don't you help us?"

"Now listen up!" The dwarf drew himself up to his full height. Unfortunately for him, this wasn't very high and brought him about level with the woman's waistband. "We are just here doing honest business. No laws against that. You're not slaves. It's the king's freedom. I'm not forcing you to work here – you could–"

"Not forcing?" shrieked the woman. "You might not have a whip to our backs, but we have nothing. No food, no homes – nothing. My husband is gone because of this silly war you started. We have no choice but to work for you. And you dare to claim that this is the king's freedom! If the king were still here, he would never put up with this. Well, I've had enough. I'd rather starve than take the pitiful amount you are offering. You can keep your *penny* – your blood money!"

The woman threw the sword onto the ground and, straight-backed and proud, she marched away.

Stunned silence hung over the group. The red-faced dwarf cleared his throat.

"Well? What are you all looking at? We're here for one more hour, then we are gone. Last chance to earn some money unless you are too proud and want to starve too."

In ones and twos, the pitiful people returned to searching for valuables on the battlefield. Jonah turned to a boy who was probably a couple of years older than him. He was skinny with a grubby face but looked friendly.

"What's the king's freedom?" Jonah asked.

The boy looked him up and down as if he were stupid.

"The king's freedom? Everyone knows that. It's been the law here for as long as anyone remembers. It means no one can force someone else to work or make them a slave. Everyone in Presadia is meant to be equal. But when the village was destroyed, we didn't have a choice. It's work for the dwarfs or starve! Here, why are you dressed all funny?"

Jonah looked down at himself. His clothes *did* stand out. His jeans and smart blue shirt – his mum always made him wear a shirt when they went to church – didn't look much like any he had seen since coming through the mirror. The only similarity was how dirty and torn they now were. The journey through the tunnel, the castle siege – and the muddy woods and fields – had not been kind to his clothes. In fact, his mum was going to be mad when she saw them. *If* he ever found his way back to the church – and his mum – and everything else that was normal. Thinking about that brought the fear back to his throat and he had to swallow hard.

"What's that?" the grumpy dwarf, who had been hovering nearby, snapped. His greedy eyes had caught sight of the axe.

"It's mine," said Jonah. "I found it."

The dwarf attempted to look casual. "I might be able to give you a few pennies for it," he offered.

Jonah's new friend looked indignant. "A few pennies? You have to be joking! That's worth more than your whole wagonload!"

A flash of annoyance crossed the dwarf's face. He glared at the boy.

"Nonsense. It looks fancier than it is. Probably couldn't even cut bread with it. Besides, it's only worth as much as someone wants to pay for it. Who else are you going to sell it to? One silver piece, and that's my final offer."

The dwarf looked longingly at the axe. Jonah's friend snorted.

"He could get a dozen gold pieces easy if he walked to Brookford. Probably two, and he'd still be selling cheap."

An idea struck Jonah.

"Have you seen a girl?" he asked the dwarf. "About this high, and wearing a white dress? She went off with some other dwarfs."

The dwarf shook his head.

"We've been here all day and not seen any girl like that. Seven silver pieces, and you're robbing me."

"Done."

The dwarf looked surprised, then smug. But as he opened a red velvet purse, Jonah added: "On one condition."

The dwarf glared at him. "What?"

"First, you have to help me find my friend. She left with some dwarfs who sold weapons to the castle."

The dwarf thought about it, then nodded.

"That will be Salt and his boys. Lord Raven and his men are so desperate, they will give anything for some good supplies. Shouldn't be difficult if your friend is with them. I can't imagine Salt will have hung about. He'll probably be heading home as we speak. You'll need to come back on the wagon with us tonight. Now, hand over the axe."

"I keep it until I find her."

The dwarf looked annoyed but relented with a grunt.

8

VAL-CHASAR

The mighty chasm of Val-Chasar truly was a sight to behold.

As they approached the base of the mountains, the wide paved road cut straight and flat through the foothills. The hillsides rose higher and higher until the ponies were trotting through an impressive straight-edged gorge. It clearly wasn't natural, and Summer could only imagine how much time it must have taken for the dwarfs to cut such a big corridor through solid rock without diggers or trucks or all the things people would use in her world.

As Summer and her dwarfish escort continued, she noticed windows and doors carved into the rock face. Dwarfs milled about, hurrying across the road on errands or chatting together in small groups. A metal sign hung over one door with a picture of a red-nosed dwarf on it. Underneath were tables where dwarfs were sitting, laughing and chinking metal goblets.

She had assumed this was the mighty chasm Salt had talked about, but unexpectedly the gorge suddenly opened up. The sides, which had been only a stone's throw apart, suddenly widened to the length of a football pitch. Before Summer and her companions, the road stopped in a large paved plaza, the far end of which dropped away. As they neared the edge, she realized they were on a giant balcony, looking out over a huge canyon that fell for hundreds of metres below them.

Along the chasm, platforms were carved from the cliff face, each topped with heroic statues of dwarfs. The cliff faces were filled with windows and doorways, walkways and staircases. Summer watched in amazement as a basket, travelling from one side of the chasm to the other on a sagging length of rope, swung back and forth dangerously.

The chasm was criss-crossed with bridges: some were terrifyingly long rope bridges that swayed as dwarfs went about their business; others were a mass of wooden beams that reminded Summer of an old wooden roller coaster she had once seen. Most impressive were the occasional stone bridges, elegantly tall arches that rose gracefully over the chaos. Those were big enough to allow heavily loaded carts to travel back and forth across the tremendous drop, pulled by other teams of long-haired ponies. There was even an aqueduct – a wide bridge that carried a fast-flowing river from one side to the other, complete with barges piled high with gravel.

Salt led their little group down a long wooden ramp that hugged one of the cliff faces. The wall at their side was carved with elaborate scenes of dwarfs doing all kinds of different things: some waving swords and axes, some on thrones, some fighting, some simply eating or sleeping. It looked to Summer like the historical timelines they had made at school, but a hundred times grander and all painted in bright colours, and decorated with gold leaf and beautiful jewels.

The city, for Val-Chasar clearly was a city, was a hive of activity, and noisy too. There were other wagons and ponies on the ramps and plazas that clung to the cliffs. Dwarfs shouted greetings to Salt and his companions or tried to sell their wares from small roadside booths. Summer was so busy looking around that it took her a moment to notice that most of their party had dispersed and that Antimony was nervously addressing her.

"Erm. Sorry, my... erm... your highness. Salt is just seeing to the wagons. He suggested we meet him outside the high lord's palace."

"The high lord? Who is he?"

"The high lord – the high ruler – is the one in charge. His beard is the most magnificent of all dwarfs'. Ruler of the Mountain Heart, Protector of the Treasury, Refiner of the Dwarfish Race..." Antimony recited the long list of titles in an unnaturally solemn voice. "... Keeper of the Seven Chests, and Bearer of the Chasm Crown, the Majestic and Mighty Tin."

Antimony paused, watching Summer for her awed reaction. He was clearly disappointed with her blank expression.

"Did you say he's called *Tin*? That doesn't sound like a very majestic name!"

"*Tin* is a very fine name for a dwarf, my lady!" Antimony huffed.

"I'm sure it is," she replied hastily, not wanting to offend her hosts. "I apologize if I sounded rude. I am still learning the way of dwarfs."

"No offence taken, my lady," said Antimony with a forgiving smile that assured her of his goodwill, "but we should really head over there. I don't want Salt to be angry at me."

Antimony had already dismounted and handed his reins to an even-smaller-than-usual dwarf. His beard was much shorter and it suddenly struck Summer that this was probably a dwarf child. Trying to hide her surprise, she tried dismounting herself. Unglamorously, she tumbled from the pony's back and flushed with gratitude for Antimony, who helped catch her. Antimony gave the small dwarf a tiny gemstone, and with a chirpy smile, the dwarf-child whisked the ponies away into the throng, leaving Summer and Antimony alone.

Antimony was a good deal faster than the other dwarfs due to his long gangly legs, but Summer was never in fear of losing him in the crowds. He stood head, shoulders, and chest above the other dwarfs. They were clearly used to his tallness, however, and a few greeted him warmly as he strode along. Summer was received with friendly but inquisitive looks as she scurried along behind him.

"Antimony…" Summer panted as she tried to keep pace, "you said that the high lord's beard was the most magnificent."

"I did indeed, my lady. You'll see it soon. It's the longest beard of any dwarf in the kingdom, by at least three handbreadths!"

"Is it the length that makes it magnificent?"

Antimony glanced down at her with a look of disbelief. "Surely, my lady, you know the importance of a dwarf's beard? You must have dwarfs in your own land."

"No. I don't think we do. At least, I haven't met any of them. Why are beards so important?"

"A beard is everything! It shows the wealth of your household; it's a sign of wisdom and honour, of success and good reputation." He spoke as if reciting a well-learned lesson. "The dwarfs with the longest beards can join the inner council, and the dwarf with the longest beard of all becomes high ruler; until someone else with a longer beard takes their place, that is."

"Why does a beard mean someone should be in charge?"

"You really don't know much about dwarfs at all, do you?" He took a deep breath, and much as if he were a teacher spelling out a simple problem to a particularly slow child, he explained: "The treasure and wealth of the dwarfs is divided up, based on beard length. The longer your beard, the bigger your share. The high ruler has the longest beard. This means he or she has the largest share. It's only natural that they should be in charge."

"So how long is the high lord's beard?" Summer asked, baffled by this strange system. Why should one dwarf be more important and have all the rewards, just because their beard happened to grow longer than another dwarf's? The way someone looks shouldn't make them more important or valuable than anyone else.

"At the last measuring, it stretched the entire width of his banqueting hall," said Antimony with obvious admiration.

"Gosh! That *must* be long!" Summer agreed.

"Yes. One day I will have a beard that long too."

Antimony sounded confident, but Summer looked at him doubtfully. His spotty chin boasted only a few sparse, fluffy hairs.

"I'm sure you will." She added as much conviction as she could into her reply but he still seemed to sense her uncertainty.

"My mother says I'm just a late bloomer. Her beard didn't come through properly until she was nearly thirty, and my Pa says that my beard is probably due a growth spurt any time. I reckon it's why I'm so tall. More room for my beard to grow."

Summer wasn't convinced that was why he was so tall, but she decided to keep her doubts to herself.

"I've been calculating how quickly my beard is growing. Only a couple of months ago I had nothing. Now my longest beard hair is almost as long as my fingernail. If it keeps growing at this rate – and taking into account the inevitable growth spurts – I'll have the longest beard by the time I am two hundred and fifty–"

"Two hundred and fifty!" exclaimed Summer. "Surely you won't live that long…"

"It is quite old, I'll give you that, but some dwarfs reach three hundred. Of course, if I got to that age, my beard would be…" Antimony started mumbling sums under his breath as they continued their walk.

They had reached a long expanse of steps that climbed up to a pair of particularly impressive doors, wide enough that fifty dwarfs could have walked through, side by side, had they been open. As it was, only a very small, dwarf-sized door, set within the larger door, stood open. A colourfully dressed guard slouched beside it.

"Is the high lord scary?" Summer asked, in an effort to steer the conversation away from the mathematics of beard growth.

Standing before the imposing door, she was suddenly feeling nervous.

"What? Scary?" Antimony looked amused. "Not at all! He's a very good high lord. He's my mother's brother's wife's fourth cousin. We are very close. I think he's Salt's grandmother's sister's eighth nephew by marriage, which makes me Salt's great-grand-cousin by marriage on my uncle's in-laws' side. Practically brothers! Now, I have a funny story about our great-grand—"

"A thousand apologies, Princess Summer!" A red-faced Salt rushed up the steps, to Summer's relief.

With his usual boisterousness, Salt pushed past them and led them to the small door.

As it happened, the door guard was – as Antimony helpfully explained – Salt's father's great-aunt's cousin's grandson. He ushered them in with a cheery greeting and a slap on Salt's back. Summer hurried after, and Antimony followed, folding himself comically through the small door.

9

THE DWARF LORD

"Ahhh! Antimony! My cousin's husband's sister's son!"

The plump dwarf was richly dressed in what Summer could only compare to an extravagant and voluminous dressing gown. Outrageously bright colours clashed and warred for attention, almost distracting from the many glittering adornments that were sewn into the clothing itself. Around his portly waist was a plaited belt with cords of gold, silver, and black, and on his big feet were burgundy velvet slippers.

His silvery beard was, as Antimony had described, magnificent. It was incredibly long and wrapped around him so many times that it looked as if some kind of hairy animal had been laid over his shoulders. Lots of shining beads and bits of jewellery were woven into it; so many, in fact, that he could have filled a couple of treasure chests. Summer was surprised he could even move under all the weight.

"How under earth are you?" went on the plump dwarf. "And Salt, my old friend. It is certainly good to see you. It's been a while. How's your grandmother doing?"

"Still putting the gran in granite," Salt laughed cheerfully.

"Wonderful! Wonderful! You must tell me how the weapons sales went over at Lord Raven's place. I had a shipment of my finest chain mail in one of your wagons. Hoping for a good profit. And I'm glad you are here, Antimony. No one can balance a ledger as well as you and I have a particularly tricky ledger I need to... But excuse me for discussing business when you clearly have a guest with you."

"Indeed I have." Salt drew himself up importantly. "It is my pleasure to introduce Princess Summer, who is visiting from a far-off land. She was caught up in an awful battle, so I took it upon myself to rescue her."

The High Lord, Ruler of the Mountain Heart, Protector of the Treasury, Refiner of the Dwarfish Race, Keeper of the Seven Chests, and Bearer of the Chasm Crown, the Majestic and Mighty Tin, beamed happily at Summer.

"A princess! My, my! Welcome, welcome, welcome!"

Summer attempted her best curtsy. "I am honoured, High Lord Tin..."

"Ruler of the Mountain Heart, Protector of..." Antimony mumbled at her without moving his lips.

"R-Ruler of the–" she stuttered.

"Nonsense, nonsense. No need for you to worry with all those fancy titles, my dear. You are a princess – royalty, nonetheless! To you, my lady, I am simply Tin."

"... the Majestic and Mighty," Antimony mumbled again.

"Antimony, please!" Tin scolded. "As I said, simply Tin."

"It's a pleasure to meet you, Tin." Summer smiled at the cheerful high lord.

"Now please, Princess Summer. Come and join me and tell me all about yourself and your far-off kingdom."

Summer's initial butterflies subsided as the evening went on. To begin with it had felt very awkward trying to maintain her lie about being a princess. Fortunately, like Salt, Tin was highly talkative and seemed content for Summer to say comparatively little.

He was an excellent host and in no time, Summer had been offered some unusual flat cakes and a goblet of warm golden drink that was quite possibly the most delicious thing she had ever tasted. He strolled with her around the underground palace, pointing out notable carvings and particularly beautiful or large gemstones in cushioned cabinets.

They ended the evening in a charming room with a large table. There were places set for four and the table was bending under the weight of the various dishes. In the corner, a group of dwarfish minstrels used silver sticks to bash stones in a rhythmic beat – something Tin referred to as "rock music".

Salt and Antimony joined them for the meal. Tin entertained them all with stories of famous dwarfs throughout history as well as their own childhoods, from Great Potash, the first dwarf ruler, to Lazuli, the famous heroine whose adventures around Presadia were clearly a highlight of dwarfish history.

It was such a delightful evening, in fact, that Summer almost forgot the strangeness of her situation and the worry about getting home. Instead she laughed and gasped as the cheerful dwarfs bantered and bragged with the familiarity of family.

"… and when Salt's mother caught us, she was so angry that she threatened to chop off his beard!" Tin roared with laughter and everyone, including Summer, joined in.

"But we have spoken enough about ourselves. Princess Summer, tell us, how did you come to be in Presadia and in such a dangerous situation?"

Summer hesitated. The dwarfs had been so good to her, it seemed wrong to tell them any more lies. They already believed she was a princess when she wasn't. But the best thing, she decided, was to tell them the truth about how she had got here. So she told them how she had discovered the secret passage and the mysterious mirror; how she had stumbled through into the castle and not been able to get back; how she had found herself in the middle of the siege. And as she related everything that had happened, it was as if a weight lifted from her shoulders.

By the time she had finished, the three dwarfs were watching her with grave expressions on their faces.

"Well, well, well, my dear," said Tin, after a pause. "It is a strange tale you tell, but I have heard stranger. You are in a somewhat tricky situation. I fear there will not be much of the castle left, and I doubt very much that your mirror door will still be there. It seems you're stuck down the mine without a lantern. Your parents, the king and queen of England, must be missing you very much. And as for your serving boy, Jonah, well – I can only imagine he is in hot magma over this."

Summer blushed. Most of what she had told the dwarfs had been the straightforward truth, but she had needed to reinforce her status as a royal princess if she were to be sure of their continued help and respect, and she was sure Jonah would forgive her once he understood the circumstances.

The door opened and a serving girl, a young dwarf with a pretty ginger beard, entered the room.

"My lord, sorry to interrupt your evening, but there is a young beggar boy demanding to see you."

Tin looked at the serving dwarf with surprise.

"A beggar boy, did you say?"

"Yes, my lord. A human. He came in with one of the scavenging wagons."

"Well, I can't very well see a beggar boy now! I'm entertaining an important princess!" He gestured toward Summer.

The attention and honour that Tin had lavished on her all evening had made Summer feel very pleased with herself. She sat up straighter and bestowed a condescending smile on the wide-eyed servant girl.

"No, no, no. Send him away and tell him to come back tomorrow, if he must. Now, where was I?"

"I'm sorry, my lord, but he's very insistent."

"Really, Jade! I can't have him in here. He's probably smelly and dirty. Princess Summer would never want to see that."

There was the sound of shouting outside the door. A grubby boy, with mud all over his face and clothes, crashed into the room, two embarrassed servants hard on his heels.

"I'm sorry, my lord… He pushed past us!"

"Jonah!" Summer shrieked, standing up so quickly she knocked her goblet over.

"Summer!" Jonah pulled up short in surprise. "What are you doing here? They wouldn't let me in because there's an important princess somewhere."

"Jonah? This is your serving boy?" Tin looked confused.

"Serving boy?" Jonah fixed Summer with an accusing look.

"Very bad manners for a serving boy…" Antimony mumbled.

"I'm not a serving boy!" protested Jonah.

Summer blushed.

"I'm… *I'm* the princess," she confessed, embarrassed at how well she had been treated by the dwarfs while poor Jonah hadn't even been allowed to enter the room.

"The princess? You're kidding, right? You're not a princess!" His confusion turned to hurt. "I came all this way to try and get help to find you, and I've been treated like dirt and told I couldn't see the high lord because there's an important princess here. And all the time…" He broke off, shaking his head in disbelief.

"I didn't mean–" she began, but he interrupted her, exploding angrily.

"It's been a nightmare!"

"Jonah, listen…"

"And all the time they're pushing me around and trying to throw me out, you're sitting here, eating and drinking and having a lovely time!"

The dwarfs watched in stunned silence, heads swivelling from one to the other, as if watching a tennis match.

"I'm sorry, Jonah! They said you were just a beggar. If I'd known it was you—"

"If you'd known it was me? So, it's fine to push a beggar boy around, is it? You're as bad as these dwarfs! And what's with all this princess stuff? You're not a princess!"

Summer's cheeks burned hot. Was it too late to own up? Maybe she should try to keep up her story. But Jonah's outburst had confused her hosts, who were mumbling among themselves. She had no choice but to own up.

"I'm sorry… I just… I liked being the princess. Even though it wasn't true…" She raised her eyes to her perplexed hosts and gave a small, embarrassed shrug. "I'm sorry. I thought you'd think I was more important if I told you I was a princess…" Tears pricked in her eyes and her voice shook as she turned to Tin.

"Tin, sorry. High lord, I'm sorry I lied about being a princess. I just felt so lost and scared, and Salt assumed I was… I didn't want to tell you the truth, in case you wouldn't help me. And I liked feeling important. Everyone was being so nice to me. You wouldn't have welcomed me if you'd thought I was just a nobody…"

"Stop. Please, stop." Tin spoke quietly but with a firmness that ensured no argument.

Summer lowered her eyes, suddenly afraid of the consequences of her lie.

10

THE DWARF'S DEEDS

"Stop. Please, stop."

The room was completely silent. All eyes were focused on Tin. Jonah's legs were shaking with emotion as he tried to contain the press of tears. No. He had to concentrate. He braced himself for an explosion of anger, frantically trying to work out how he and Summer might make their escape.

How many dwarfs were there? He still had the golden axe, strapped to his back with filthy rags from the battlefield. Maybe he could fight his way out... But he had never swung an axe or had to fight before.

Jonah wondered what dwarfs did when they lost their temper. He was pretty near the end of his!

It had been the worst afternoon of his life. His dangerous escape from the castle had left him scared, shaken, and alone. His trek across the countryside, followed by the bumpy wagon ride squeezed uncomfortably among the dwarfs' loot, had left him grubby, tired, bruised, and aching.

At Val-Chasar he had been laughed and sneered at, rudely dismissed by the dwarfs in the palace, despite his protests that he wasn't a beggar. They had tried to throw him out, and it was only by convincing his escort that he wouldn't hand over the golden axe until he had spoken with the high lord himself that he had finally been allowed entry to the palace.

He had had no luck getting an audience with the dwarfish leader, however, since he was apparently busy entertaining an important foreign princess. Eventually he had given up trying to persuade anyone and resorted to ducking past the guards and forcing his way through the door, only to find out that the high-and-mighty princess was none other than Summer. That had been the final straw.

He had been sick with worry about her, risked his life and been looked down on, only to find that all the while she had been having a great time, laughing and feasting and enjoying herself with dwarf lords, and thinking of herself as oh-so-important! His anger warred with his desire to simply burst into tears at everything that had happened.

"Stop," said the dwarf lord again. "It is I who should be saying sorry." He hung his head. "You are right. I would not have welcomed you here, or sought to impress and look after you so well, had I known you were not a princess. But that is *my* wrongdoing. For you are just as valuable and important as any princess, no matter who you are. I must beg your forgiveness, Princess Sum... Summer." He turned to Jonah. "And to you, I must beg even more forgiveness. I should not have shown such favouritism by looking down on you as less worthy than a princess. That is not how we dwarfs like to live. We remember the old ways, the king's ways, and everyone is welcome at my table. Please join us."

Jonah was taken aback by the dwarf's apology. He hadn't expected him to be sorry, or the sudden kindness. But Jonah's anger was already boiled up and he needed to release it at someone.

All he could think about was the suffering of the homeless villagers, the hungry children and the angry widow, and the way the dwarfs were taking advantage of them. He couldn't look on the grand banqueting hall and lavishly decorated dwarfs without seeing the faces of the poor people they had practically enslaved. This dwarf lord might seem generous and kindly spoken in his own palace, but how could Jonah accept that when he had seen how the dwarfs exploited the poor villagers? It was all just too unfair.

"No! You treated me awfully because you thought I was a beggar! You sit here, feasting and laughing, while your dwarfs are bullying poor people whose homes and lives have been destroyed by the wars that you started. You are rich – but only because you take advantage of those who are too poor to do anything else. You don't care if others starve, as long as you can get fat!" He was sobbing now. "I thought I was going to die in that castle. They were right – the women I met. You claim to follow the ways of your old king; you claim to uphold 'the king's freedom' – but it's all a lie! I've seen it. The people out there are like slaves. They have no choice but to work for you and you don't even pay them enough so that they can eat. They said the king would never have put up with this! You sound all nice and kind and reasonable, but it's all built on other people's misery – just so you can be comfortable."

"We are followers of the king," protested Tin, shock and hurt in his voice.

"No! You say you are. You say you are followers of the king, but if that's how his followers behave and treat people… well, he must be a pretty awful king."

The dwarfs gasped. Jonah stood panting, his anger spent. The room was uncomfortably silent after his outburst, and he realized he had been shouting at full volume. He knew he shouldn't have; he should have accepted the dwarf's offer to join them at the table. But it all seemed so unfair and false. He glared at his feet, willing himself to stop crying and ready for the high lord's wrath or the appearance of palace guards.

There was nothing. Just a long, long pause.

Jonah breathed deeply, regaining control of himself. Hesitantly, he lifted his head to look at the dwarf lord. The last of his anger melted away as he saw the horrified expression on the dwarfish leader's rosy face.

Tears welled in his amber eyes and streaked down his cheeks, disappearing into his silver beard. Looking around, Jonah saw the other dwarfs were similarly stunned. They looked blank with horror as they were confronted with the dark truth behind their comfortable lives and luxurious possessions.

Still no one spoke.

Jonah shuffled his feet. "Come on, Summer. Let's go."

He turned to leave, then hesitated as he recalled his bargain. Slipping the makeshift strap holding the golden axe from his back, he walked back to the head dwarf and placed it on the ground in front of him, the dirty rag it was wrapped in falling away. Tin stared wide-eyed at the beautiful axe, dumbfounded.

"Oh, I almost forgot. I traded this to a dwarf to find Summer. He can keep the coins. I just want to go home." Jonah made his way toward the door again. Summer followed him, looking awkward and unsure.

Tin's voice broke the silence. As if talking to himself, he read aloud the words on the axe handle:

> *Live your words and don't just speak;*
> *Protect the poor, defend the weak.*
> *Beliefs are dead when missing deeds;*
> *To speak and do is what we need.*

Jonah had reached the door. His anger had died but he felt a sadness and a disappointment in the dwarfs. They didn't seem like bad people, but they were blind to the suffering their lifestyle caused. Their brave words and noble claims fell flat in the face of their actions. He raised his hand to the door latch.

"Wait," Tin called after him. "Please, wait."

Jonah stopped, not turning around.

"You are right. I... I never really thought about it. It isn't that I want these people to suffer, I just..." Tin struggled for words. "No. There's no excuse. Jonah, you have shone a light onto an area of our lives that we have ignored for too long. You are right. We cannot claim... *I* cannot claim to be a king's dwarf when my actions don't match my words.

"Salt, go out and gather as many dwarfs as you can. This ends right now. Tonight. Tell them to gather tools, wagons, supplies, and anything else they might need. We have a responsibility. We must rebuild the villages and help those who have lost their homes and families. Also, send a messenger to the siege at Lord Raven's castle. Get them to do whatever they can to broker peace. And Antimony, use that brain of yours to chew over the mathematics and see if you can work out a way to compensate everyone who has not been treated fairly.

"Jade." The forgotten serving girl straightened in surprise as the high lord addressed her. "Prepare the guest rooms. All of them. Anyone who is without a home or somewhere to sleep must come here. Send servants to all the other homes in Val-Chasar and tell them to do the same. And send for the scribes. I will write a letter to be read aloud all over Val-Chasar. Hurry now, all of you, and do as I say."

The dwarfs burst into a flurry of activity as they jumped to obey their leader.

Salt, bafflement and excitement battling on his face, bounded past Jonah and Summer to follow Tin's directions.

"Salt! Wait," Summer called, suddenly remembering something. She pulled the pretty ring from her finger and thrust it into the dwarf's hands. "I took this from the castle. I shouldn't have – it's not mine."

"Never fear, your high… Summer. I shall ensure it is returned."

With that, Salt hurried out, leaving Summer and Jonah alone with High Lord Tin.

"Jonah, Summer, I owe you a great debt. You have taught me a difficult lesson today. You have shown me the error of our people and my own part in it. Jonah, this axe will remain with you. You have proven by your bravery in speaking up that you are worthy of bearing such a weapon.

"I have searched long and hard for this axe. I had given up hope of ever finding it. Your bringing it here today and reminding me of its inscription is too much of a coincidence for me to ignore. It is worth far more than a few coins. *I* will pay the dwarf you bargained with, but you must keep this and remember the lesson inscribed upon it. I know *I* will not forget those words again soon!"

He reverently picked up the axe from the floor and walked toward Jonah, solemnly handing it over. Jonah took it silently, somewhat overawed by Tin's dramatic response to his accusations. He had never expected the dwarf to respond with such remorse and conviction.

Tin's eyes were still welling with tears as he gazed upon the beautiful weapon in Jonah's hands. The axe was clearly hugely significant to the remorseful dwarf. He had been stunned and hurt by Jonah's revelations, but it was upon seeing the axe that something within him had shifted.

"No," Jonah said, looking Tin in the eye. "You should take it. I don't know how to use an axe and it's too big for me, anyway."

The dwarf gazed at the axe with an expression of wonderment.

"Words cannot express…" He looked Jonah in the eyes. "Thank you. It is truly a kingly gift. I will bear it with gladness, as a symbol and reminder of today. But you must tell me, is there any way in which the dwarfs can aid you? I would willingly give it."

Jonah frowned, unsure what to say.

"Home," Summer said quietly. "We need to go home."

"The mirror's broken," Jonah told her, at a loss as to what they should do next. The need to hold himself together had fuelled him since passing through the mirror. He had been so intent on finding Summer – and so distressed at what the dwarfs had done – that he hadn't had time to think too far ahead. Now that was done, he felt completely lost. All he wanted was to get home to his family. He felt scared and out of his depth. Adventures were all very well in his imagination or in stories, but the reality was very different. Eleven years old didn't feel so grown up any more.

"I do not pretend to know about this magic mirror of yours, or how we will get you home, but I promise the help of the dwarfs of Val-Chasar in this quest. We will do whatever we can to help, however long it takes."

"But what can we do? We're stuck here," said Summer, a note of desperation in her voice.

Tin frowned thoughtfully, "There is one thing I can think of, or at least one person. If anyone knows how to get you home, it will be her."

"Who?" Jonah asked.

Tame your tongue and watch your words,
For they have power when said or heard.
They choose your steps and steer your feet,
And reap a harvest, sour or sweet.

11

Khoree's Lair

"Wise Khoree, Heart-of-the-Mountain, we come seeking your counsel," Tin called as loudly as it was possible while still sounding respectful.

The sudden wave of heat that rolled from the cave hit Summer's numb face, making her eyes water.

The journey up and up, higher and higher, into the rugged mountain peaks had been difficult and long. It had taken three days, with the nights spent in colourful tents, on beds of soft fur. The temperature had dropped the higher they climbed. As they wove in single file up the winding mountain paths the ride had chilled Summer to the bone, despite the thick fur coat the dwarfs had given her; she had been jealous of the ponies' long hair and the dwarfs' warm beard-scarves. Antimony, who was also lacking on the beard front, had shown her how to turn up the big fluffy collar of her coat to shield herself from some of the biting wind.

The final part of the journey had been made on foot. The ponies, despite any number of soothing words or pearl-handled brushes, had refused to come the final few hundred metres after hearing the first roar. It had shaken the ground and Summer had thought at first it must be the rumble of thunder. As they had neared their destination, a second bone-shaking groan had struck awe and terror into her.

The heat waves funnelled out of the cave, causing the large area in front of it to be clear of snow or plant life. The dwarfs – Tin, Salt, Antimony, and a dozen other half-cousins and distant nephews – shuffled nervously from foot to foot and muttered to each other as they looked at the cave mouth.

The ground shook again with a thunderous sound, like the crashing of waterfalls or the rumble of an avalanche, echoing from the dark cave.

"Who disturbs me?"

"I am Tin, high lord of the dwarfs. I bring two human children, Summer and Jonah, who have come from a strange and distant land–"

"Children? Children! You disturb my misery for children? I am almost as old as time itself! What concerns of children could be important to me?" The heat from the cave intensified as the voice grew angrier. "Agghhh!"

The final sound was something between a sneeze and a shout of frustration and was lost in a roar of fire. From the depths of the cave a ball of flame exploded, banishing the darkness for a few seconds. Summer heard Jonah gasp.

In the flash of the fireball, they had caught a glimpse of the largest creature she had ever seen. Blue scales glittered with ten thousand reflections of the ruby flames and ran in flowing curves over muscled limbs. A long, serpentine neck, immensely powerful and yet at the same time graceful, was punctuated with vicious spines and led to an elegant head with two enormous eyes that glowed with mesmerising brilliance. Slitted pupils, like a snake's, divided jewelled irises that shone like molten amber.

The fireball sputtered. The cave fell into darkness once more.

Summer let go of the breath she hadn't realized she was holding.

"Agghhh! Be gone, dwarf! Irritate me no more with your trivial concerns. Leave me in peace."

"It sounds very angry," Jonah muttered to her.

Its scales cracking like a hundred whips, the creature erupted from the cave mouth into the light, billows of smoke belching from its nostrils. A growl that could be felt more than heard vibrated through Summer's bones. The ferocious head stopped centimetres from Jonah's face.

Summer and the dwarfs scrambled backwards in fear. Looking behind her, she saw Jonah flat on his back and frozen in fear as the dragon sniffed him scornfully. Its huge, hostile eyes surveyed him.

"*It?* Did no one ever teach you to speak respectfully to a dragon, boy?"

Jonah, petrified with fear, couldn't speak.

"I am nearly as old as time itself; you are but a fly... inconsequential. Here only for a moment. You do not know what it is to live for millennia, to live in pain, and know that pain will continue for eternity. Do I sound angry?" The dragon's breath grew hotter and hotter, the waves of heat that pulsed out forcing Summer to back away even further. Jonah had no such defence. Desperately trying to shield his face from the heat, he wriggled frantically in a vain attempt to escape the furious dragon's gaze.

"I *am* angry, boy. Angrier than you can conceive. My anger has multiplied over thousands of years. I... I..." With another mighty roar, the dragon raised her head into the air, fire mushrooming from her snarling mouth and forked tongue.

"Mighty Khoree!" Tin's voice was high with nervousness. "Earnestly I beg your patience and mercy! These humans know little of dragons or any of the ways of this kingdom. No offence was intended, I am certain."

With lightning speed, Khoree whipped her head around until she was face to face with Tin. The brave dwarf somehow remained steady, not even flinching. Salt, on the other hand, leaped back with a high squeak, knocking over Antimony – who, in turn, took out several other dwarfs like bowling pins. They all scrabbled hastily to their feet and retreated to a safer distance. Tin remained alone, bravely facing the dragon's wrath.

"Then he should not have spoken!"

"I'm sorry – I didn't think before speaking," Jonah apologized, jumping thankfully to his feet and hurrying back to Summer's side.

"Thoughtless words wound as deeply as swords," Khoree growled.

"But wisely spoken words bring healing," put in Tin, grasping the opportunity. "It is for your wise words that we come to you. These children do not belong here. They stumbled into our kingdom through a magical mirror. But the mirror's broken. We come for advice as to how to get them home again."

"A fine story, dwarf," said Khoree in a resentful grumble. Even her grumble was enough to make Summer's hair stream out behind her and cause a distant pony to whinny anxiously. "A mirror, you say? Interesting. I once knew of many mirrors like the one you speak of. All were destroyed many, many centuries ago. Or so I thought."

The dragon fell into a thoughtful silence, thin plumes of smoke wisping from her mighty nostrils. After an uncomfortably long pause, in which it became apparent Khoree didn't intend to elaborate further, Summer swallowed and spoke up.

"So... can you help us? Please? If one mirror survived, maybe others did? We need to get home. Our parents don't know where we are and will be terribly worried about us."

Khoree slowly swung her reptilian head in Summer's direction, fixing her with an unreadable and unblinking gaze. Looking into her eyes was like looking into time itself; endlessly deep and ancient, unfathomably wise and yet tinged with a weariness and pain that made Summer feel a sudden sympathy for her.

"Why are you in pain?"

Beside her, the dwarfs froze in horror.

Khoree stared at Summer, her cold, yellow eyes giving away nothing.

"What is your name, girl?" she asked, her voice dropping to a volume that was almost bearable, and – for the first time – free from anger.

"Summer."

"Summer. A lovely name. It reminds me of long days and being lifted by the warmth of the air to soar over the green land and glittering water. A good name."

"Thank you." Summer blushed.

"You, Summer, are the only one ever to ask me that question. I have lived here for thousands of years. Generations of dwarfs, elves, and humans have come seeking to steal my wisdom and leech my knowledge, yet none have cared enough to ask me. For that, I thank you. Now, you have asked a question, so I will ask you one. If you answer wisely, then I will help you."

12

A Dragon's Riddle

Raising herself up to her full height, Khoree flexed her muscles. Her blue scales shimmered like chain mail. She settled herself down and surveyed Summer, Jonah, and the party of dwarfs.

> *I am small, but I steer the whole;*
> *I seem unremarkable, and yet I set your course;*
> *I am tiny, yet I make great boasts;*
> *No one has tamed me –*
> *If they could, they would be perfect.*
> *What am I?*

Summer frowned, thinking hard.

"May my friends help me?" she asked.

"It is wise to seek the advice of others when you need it. You may," said Khoree.

"Summer, I have a suggestion," Tin spoke up. "At first I thought it might be a beard. After all, there is the bit about taming it and becoming perfect! But then I realized it didn't fit with steering the whole and setting the course. That got me thinking. The traders sail big ships up and down the rivers and across the oceans. Those huge ships are steered by a tiny rudder. Using that, the captain can take the boat wherever he wants."

"A good suggestion, dwarf, but incorrect," said Khoree with a grunt.

"I know!" Jonah said excitedly. "It's the ponies! You know, like the ones we rode up the mountain. Or rather, it's the little bits in their mouths, attached to the reins. They are tiny but they let us steer and control the ponies."

"Well tried, boy, but this thing is much harder to tame than any horse. People have tamed all kinds of animals, but no one has tamed this yet."

Summer frowned as she stared up at the dragon. Khoree yawned, turning her head sideways. Summer caught a glimpse of her forked tongue steaming in the cold air before her jaw clamped shut again. She frowned. It could have just been a yawn, but the dragon was watching her closely in a way that made her think.

"Your tongue!" she said, the answer coming to her in a sudden flash. "It's tiny but it makes big boasts and says grand things. And people say stuff they don't mean all the time; silly things and bad things. What we say *does* steer our course, doesn't it? Like just now, when Jonah made you angry, even though he didn't mean to."

"Yes!" Salt bounced up and down with excitement. "I think you're right. My mother always used to say, 'A tangled tongue will land you in more trouble than a tangled beard.'"

If dragons could have smiled, Summer knew that was what Khoree would have been doing. As it was, her eyes glittered with pleasure.

"Well done, girl. You are correct."

Summer smiled at her, but then her face became serious again. In the instant the answer had become clear to her, she had been troubled by another realization.

"Wait. Is that also the answer to my question – your tongue? Is that what's hurting you?"

Khoree gazed at her for a few moments in silence. Then she inclined her massive head.

"You are very astute, girl." She sighed. "It is the way of dragons. Our tongues burn inside our mouths. It pains me all day long. It heats my breath and sets my words on fire. That makes me angry, and my anger causes it to burn all the stronger."

"That sounds dreadful!"

The dragon seemed more sad than angry now. The hot wind from her nostrils made Summer's fringe tickle her face as it fluttered.

"You come seeking my aid to find your way back home. You have answered wisely, and you show a goodness of heart that refreshes me. I will help as much as I can. The mirror of which you spoke – once there were many in the palace of the king. They were created by the king himself. He was a true artist – more masterful than even the dwarfs. They were made with great love and he took joy in them. It is said he made them so well that their reflections were truer than those of any other type of mirror. They offered the viewer the chance to see into the very depths of themselves – to who they were and who they might be. I have heard it told that sometimes people glimpsed what seemed to be other worlds, perhaps like your own. Maybe your world is another reflection of Presadia.

"When the king was overthrown by his own servants, the palace was looted and damaged. I knew it very well, but alas, it has been many, many years since I went there. It became the centre of battles between the king's wicked servants as they fought for power, and soon not a stone was left on top of another. I had believed the mirrors, as with all the treasure of the palace, to have disappeared long ago. The stories of the king's palace, all its goodness and beauty, have faded into myth. But the loss of beauty and goodness hasn't stopped there. The entire kingdom has been withering ever since those fateful times."

The dragon's voice was low but burned with a righteous anger.

"Did they kill the king?" Jonah asked hesitantly, horror in his eyes at the sad story.

"They tried. Many think they did, but the elves helped him escape and he fled into exile. Where, I do not know. Maybe the elves still recall. What I do know is that the king has not been seen since."

"How sad," said Summer. "He must have grown old and died all alone, never seeing another person."

"He is not like you, girl. There is something of humanity in him but he also has the magic of the elves, who command nature to do their bidding. He has the creativity of the dwarfs, who craft masterpieces beyond imagination. More than that, he has the blood of dragons, who do not die." Khoree paused and her eyes grew sad. "Still, many wonder if he is indeed dead, for it has been an age since those dark days.

"He is like us, and yet not like us – or rather, we are like him, but not like him. Is he dead? In truth, I do not know. If only he still ruled, I would send you to him, for no matter how dire a situation, or how important a quest, the king always knew what to do. But... But I have failed."

The final sentence was delivered with a billow of hot smoke that made Khoree's visitors all take a step back.

"I – a dragon and a guardian of the right and the true – whose job it was to serve the king! A dragon who was tricked by mere men to be far from her king when they cast him out. They taunted and teased me until my anger exploded; until I set fire to the palace. A dragon who fled in shame rather than deal with the consequences of her actions. A dragon who feels such guilt that she has hidden in a cave for millennia, like a dog licking its wounds! A dragon... A dragon... No! Not a *true* dragon!"

The ferocity of Khoree's self-hatred stunned Summer. She stumbled fearfully backwards, away from the dragon. Smoke was pouring from her mouth with each shout as the guilt of thousands of years exploded from her, like a volcano erupting. She let out a heart-wrenching cry to the sky; fire and anguish mingled in a blinding pillar of fire that shot up twenty metres or more with terrible force.

Then, with equal suddenness, the dragon collapsed into a heap – almost pathetic, like an animal too tired to move any further.

"You come seeking my aid, but the truth is, I am not worthy of your trust."

After the thundering outburst, the silence that followed was absolute.

Tears rolled down Summer's face, drying before they hit the ground in the heat that radiated from the dragon.

"Khoree…" she whispered.

The dragon lay unmoving, but her sad eyes shifted slowly to meet Summer's.

"Khoree, they tricked you. You weren't to know."

"I should have known. And even if I could not have known, I should not have hidden like a frightened lamb. I should have found him. I should have brought him back to wreak judgment on those who betrayed him. It's too late now. I am done. I could never be forgiven for what I did. I will stay on this mountain forever. I will live out my punishment of remembering what I have done."

No one spoke.

The wind blew gently across the group; snowflakes danced around the watchers, the only movement in the otherwise desolate silence.

13

THE DRAGON'S SECRET

"No!" Tin's voice broke the spell.

"The axe… the words on the axe." Tin drew the weapon from a specially designed strap that held it to his back and glanced toward Jonah.

"This axe belonged to my great-great-great-grandmother. It was made by the king himself as a gift to her, though she was but a lowly serving girl in his palace. An extravagant and generous gift for someone so lowly. The words are a part of a song. An old, old song. It was given that we might remember its wisdom always – but alas, I fear I had forgotten it, until Jonah returned the axe to me.

"There's more to the song than the words on this handle. Your riddle – about the tongue – it reminded me…" He started to sing, his voice soaring loud and true on the silent mountain.

> *Face yourself, what do you see?*
> *Reflected back in honesty,*
> *At once, your pride and vanity,*
> *With visions of what you could be.*
>
> *Live your words and don't just speak;*
> *Protect the poor, defend the weak.*

Beliefs are dead when missing deeds;
To speak and do is what we need.

Tame your tongue and watch your words,
For they have power when said or heard.
They choose your steps and steer your feet,
And reap a harvest, sour or sweet.

His voice faltered.

"There's more, I'm sure, but... I last heard it so long ago..."

"Those were the words on the mirror!" shouted Summer, making Jonah jump with her excitement. "The first verse. They were written on the mirror frame. I read them."

Khoree lifted her head to give Summer and Tin a quizzical look.

"It is an ancient song. There *is* more, as the dwarf says. I am surprised you know it. I have not heard it for many hundreds of years."

"It is little known, even among the dwarfs," Tin admitted, "but the axe was in my family for generations until my father lost it, and my great-grandmother had a fondness for the old songs. She would sing them to me as a babe and tell me stories of the king's generosity. Often we thought she was simply making them up."

"She was not," Khoree assured him.

"Your tongue pains you, dragon, but that is not the heart of your problem. Your tongue has entrapped you more than you realize. By telling yourself you are a failure, you become one. By stating that you will never leave this mountain, you make it so. By calling yourself unforgivable, you refuse to ever be forgiven. Your words have chosen your steps and steered your course."

"Who are you to teach me, dwarf?" Khoree arched her neck dangerously.

"Does it matter who I am, if my teaching is good? Is it wrong to tell someone the right tunnel if they have wandered and become lost in the mine? These children taught me. They taught me that words alone are worthless. What we believe is demonstrated by what we do. We said we followed the king, yet our actions told a different story. You claim to have abandoned him and failed, but rather than seeking to change that through your actions, you let your words trap you here."

"It is not that simple, dwarf!"

"You are wise, dragon. It is the gift of your kind. Stop being stubborn and let your wisdom show. Don't waste your life here."

"You get above yourself, dwarf! I do not die! I have more than enough life to use as I please!"

Khoree was growing angry again, her muscles clenching, her spine arching like an alley cat preparing for a fight. Tin stood his ground, however – boldly defiant, a tiny figure next to the dragon's ferocious bulk.

"You get above yourself, dragon. You said yourself, you are a dragon, a guardian of the truth and a servant of the king."

"The king is gone!" Khoree's voice rose to a roar.

"You do not even know if he is dead. If there is even a chance that he is alive – as you say – how can you sit here doing nothing?" Tin was shouting too now, but with a firmness that gave him, thought Jonah, far more authority than the length of his beard. "Be a dragon again. Stop lying here pitying yourself. You pledged your service to the king–"

"I cannot go!" Khoree thundered, sparks and small flames licking the corners of her mouth.

Her cry echoed around the mountains, each repeat growing fainter, until silence surrounded them again.

"I cannot go," the dragon repeated, her anger under control once more.

"Why?" Jonah asked. "You know what Tin says is possible. You could help us look for the king. It sounds like he's the only one who can help us."

The dragon shuffled, ashamed and awkward. She looked to Jonah more like a guilty dog than a majestic dragon.

"I wish I could, boy."

"You can!" Jonah insisted.

"How can I go anywhere? I cannot control my own tongue. It makes me angry and sets fire to my words. I burned the king's palace in anger. I will not endanger the world by leaving this cave."

"But it was an accident. The wicked servants made you angry... you didn't mean to burn the palace."

"But I *did* burn it!" Khoree wailed.

"Dragon." Tin spoke up again. "Khoree, what if we could help you with your tongue? Would you help us in return? Would you help us search for our king and get these children back home?"

The dragon hesitated.

"If you could help me, I would willingly aid you. But... I do not believe there is a way to help me."

"You forget, mighty Khoree, about the creativity of dwarfs. How much can you carry when you fly?"

Khoree looked puzzled.

"I may be old but I remain strong."

"Then I have an idea..."

From that moment onward, the clearing in front of the cave was a buzz of activity. Tin had given instructions to his company of dwarfs, who quickly erected a campsite of colourful tents that even included a small blacksmith's workshop. Jonah didn't know where the dwarfs had produced the tools and materials from, but before long a team was sent into the surrounding woods to gather resources. Another group, led by Salt, was sent higher up the mountain on a secret mission. Jonah wasn't sure what they were looking for, but they took chisels and axes, and almost all the ponies.

He watched them stomping off through the deepening snow before turning back to the small group who had remained in the camp. The activity focused on Tin, who stood in the middle of the camp, sketching plans for whatever his idea was. From what Jonah could gather, Tin wanted to build some kind of enormous basket for Khoree, but he didn't understand how this would help the dragon with her burning tongue. He hovered near Tin for a few minutes, but the dwarfs were absorbed in sums and conversions regarding the tension and strength of various materials and the impact on aerodynamics. Antimony, it seemed, was a natural mathematician and the other dwarfs listened closely to his workings out. His rambling step-by-step calculations reminded Jonah of his complicated explanations of dwarfish family trees and he was quickly lost by their complexity.

In fact, most of the technical conversations made no sense at all to him. After trying to follow for some time, he wandered back to Khoree and Summer, who were sitting in the entrance to the cave, watching the snow fall.

Khoree had lit a small fire so Summer could warm herself. The dragon seemed to have developed a particular fondness for Summer but didn't seem to mind when Jonah joined them beside the fire.

"Dwarfs are funny," he commented, taking a seat beside Summer. "They can seem a bit silly and bumbling at times, but now I can't understand a word of what they are talking about. Antimony's sums are so complicated, he's using letters as well as numbers. I didn't think people actually did that in real life."

"An interesting 'dwarf', that one," mused Khoree. "I suspect there is more to his story than he realizes. We each have our own gifts. We are strongest when we allow others to use theirs to the best of their ability. I wonder what will come of the tall one's sums. I do not know what the dwarf lord intends, but if anyone can build something to help a fiery tongue, it is the dwarfs."

"Khoree," said Summer, "you mentioned that the king had the blood of dragons; that he lived forever. I had assumed he was a human like us for some reason."

"What gave you the impression he was a human being?" She chuckled, or at least that's what Summer thought the good-natured rumble was. "Perhaps it's not really the blood of dragons. But he is immortal like us and the elves. People always imagine he is like them. I suppose it makes it easier for us to try and understand him. That is the mistake his wicked servants made. They thought they were like him, only wiser and stronger. They thought they could do better than the king. Alas, they failed, and threw Presadia into chaos. It sounds as if many things are different in your world, but perhaps, in one way, we are the same. We find it hard to imagine that something, or someone, else can be different from our ourselves and our own experience."

"Did you know him? The king, I mean," Summer probed.

The dragon was silent for a moment.

"Yes. I knew him well. I served the king. I would take him all over Presadia. They say dragons are wise, but I learned so much from him. We would talk for hours. I was always surprised that he would spend so much time with me, but he was the best master you could ever serve."

The dragon stopped suddenly, engrossed in deep thought. Jonah listened to the crackle of the fire, the hubbub of the dwarfs, and the wind in the mountain trees.

"Do you think we will ever get home?" he asked.

He had meant the question for Summer, but it was Khoree who replied, in a reassuring rumble.

"Sometimes we don't know the destination. All we can do is put one foot in front of the other and aim in the right direction, and trust that will bring us to the proper place in the end."

"But what do we do now?" Summer asked. "What's the right step now?"

"It sounds like the king is the only one who can help us," said Jonah.

"But we don't even know if the king is alive," protested Summer.

"We don't know that he's dead either. Surely, if there's any chance that he's alive, we need to try and find him. If we're wrong, we're wrong, but it's all we have to go on."

"I believe the elves are the most likely to know where you should look," Khoree told them. "They helped the king escape when his servants turned against him. Their own queen was betrothed to the king. For a long time, they acted as stewards on his behalf to try and govern the kingdom. Their efforts failed, sadly. Then even the elves became inward-looking. The elfish queen led them into hidden places in the forests, away from the worries and troubles of the other races. The boy is right. It is a wise course of action to find out more. The elves are the obvious place to start. Maybe they can help you find the king. It would be a noble quest. One I would be honoured to help you with."

"And I!"

Summer and Jonah jumped. Tin had joined them by the fire, approaching silently out of the twilight.

"You two have been here so short a time, but already you have shaken up this kingdom more than you know. Maybe it will be a fruitless quest, but if anyone has a chance of finding the king, it is you, I'm sure."

The dwarf glanced down at the flames for a moment; their amber glow made the beads in his beard glitter like stars.

"I promise you," he lifted his eyes to theirs, suddenly very solemn, "that I will do everything I can to help you find him, whatever it takes, however far we have to travel, and whatever hardships we have to face."

Jonah didn't like the sound of that last part. He swallowed hard.

"But... what about the other dwarfs? Don't you have to stay here and be their high ruler?"

"Perhaps this is the best way *to* lead them," said Tin. "Salt has agreed to take a message back to the council of elders. They will rule in my absence. Too long have I sat in my comfortable halls, eating and drinking and living a selfish life."

"It will be good to travel with you, dwarf." Khoree grunted approvingly.

"Likewise, mighty Khoree."

There was a short, companionable pause.

"Anyway," Tin continued in a more businesslike tone, "I came to update you. We have several days of work ahead of us. Khoree, tomorrow, if you would be willing, I must measure you and see you fly."

"I will humour you, dwarf. I am willing."

"Good. Good. Well. In which case, I will call upon you in the morning. I bid you all a good night. I must get on – lots to do!"

Smiling to himself and humming a little tune, Tin hurried back to the industrious camp.

The others mused in silence for a while, watching the busyness, until a big yawn overcame Jonah.

Khoree stood and stretched before resettling herself, letting her tail wrap protectively in a loose circle around the campfire, protecting Summer and Jonah from the wind. It was as if the exhaustion of the last four days was now catching up with Jonah: the escape from the castle, the journey to Val-Chasar, and the long three-day climb through the mountains. He ached all over from riding; his mind was numbed from the constant surprises of their time in Presadia. Almost too tired to think, he slumped back against the dragon. Khoree's scales were warm and surprisingly comfortable.

In no time at all, he was fast asleep.

14

THE TONGUE-TAMER

"I don't think this was such a good idea!" Jonah shouted against the deafening wind.

He had never felt so terrified. The huge cradle the dwarfs had made swung horribly in the buffeting wind. Khoree gripped it tight in her great claws, her vast bulk looming over them.

Jonah wanted to throw up. He had never been on a big roller coaster, but he imagined this was probably ten times worse than the scariest one. Between each powerful wingbeat, the cradle – which carried him, Summer, Tin, and a massive block of ice – dropped in an alarming free fall that made his stomach lurch. Then, just when it seemed the straps holding them to Khoree's harness had given way or she had let go of the tree-trunk grip, the next flap of the dragon's wings would jerk them upward.

If he hadn't had his eyes squeezed tightly shut, Jonah would have seen the land shrinking quickly beneath them as the dragon flew higher and higher.

The cradle, which Tin and the dwarfs had nicknamed "the tongue-tamer", looked a bit like a small house with a large handle on top. The main section, at the back, housed a massive chunk of ice, chiselled by the dwarfs from a glacier high in the mountains. It was packed with dead grass and wrapped in furs to stop it melting too quickly, and at the top was a flap that could be opened to allow Khoree access to the ice. Tin had explained that Khoree could use the ice to cool down her tongue when she became angry. At first, Khoree had look unconvinced, but when she had carefully tried licking the frozen block, her whole body had relaxed and her usual short temper was considerably soothed. After that, they had had trouble separating the dragon from the ice block. Tin's solution certainly seemed to meet with the now placid dragon's approval.

At the front of "the tongue-tamer", the dwarfs had built something resembling a small balcony. It was here that Jonah, Summer and the dwarf lord huddled now, strapped in and holding on for dear life.

Tin and the dragon had tested "the tongue-tamer", with everyone else watching from the safety of solid ground. As Khoree lifted it up high into the sky, Jonah had marvelled at how little it had moved around. An ingenious system of straps, a specially crafted harness, and the dwarfs' clever design of the cradle itself had made it look remarkably stable and secure.

Watching from the ground and being strapped into the cradle, now it was suspended in the air, were two very different experiences, however. Jonah's eyes were scrunched so tight they almost hurt, and his knuckles were white as he gripped the leather straps that prevented him from falling out.

The dragon seemed to climb forever. Finally, when Jonah thought he could take no more, the sickening ascent ended, and Khoree glided smoothly on a warmer air current. Jonah dared a peep and immediately wished he hadn't. The ground was a long way below, the mountains and hills looking like miniature models. They were cloaked in the evil mist that smothered much of the landscape in all directions. Only a short way above, similar smoggy clouds with an evil yellow tinge bubbled like a cosmic cauldron of rotting stew. The air was freezing at this altitude, and Jonah had to snatch small breaths between the gusts of icy wind.

"I dare not go higher," Khoree thundered, her normally deafening voice only just audible over the wind. "The clouds above are unclean and unnatural. Even here, the air is not clean. The kingdom rots and the air is thick with its putrid stench…"

If Khoree said more, it was lost to Jonah.

They were travelling quickly. The land beneath them sped past steadily. Distances that would have taken hours on foot were crossed in minutes. Khoree preferred long curving glides, something Jonah was grateful for. The dragon's weight, combined with the heavy ice block and her three passengers, pulled her down rapidly, so Khoree had to beat her way up again between each glide.

They were heading for the Silver Wood, home to the elves and the queen who had once been betrothed to the king himself.

Jonah opened his eyes a crack to glance sideways at Tin and Summer strapped in beside him. Like him, they were holding on with all their strength, despite the straps holding them in place. Summer's eyes were squeezed shut; whether from fear or because of the wind, Jonah wasn't sure. Tin, on the other hand, had a huge grin on his face and was looking around with glee. He caught Jonah's glance.

"Oohhh yes!" he called above the roar of the wind. "This is working exceptionally! Exactly as I had planned! This is better than a barrel of diamonds. Yippeee!" The excited dwarf threw his arms and legs into the air in joyful abandon, so that all that was holding him in place were the leather straps. Jonah clamped his eyes closed again firmly. This was not his idea of a fun adventure.

They flew for hours, though the time was hard to tell for Jonah, miserable and terrified as he was. Khoree eventually glided down in huge lazy spirals. She beat her wings hard just before reaching solid ground, landing the cradle gently in a woodland clearing. Jonah was feeling quite sick and chilled to the bone. The dragon herself had to land awkwardly so as not to trample the cradle or drag it through the trees by the straps connected to her harness, but after a few quick beats of her wings and some ungainly hopping about, she shook out her wings and folded them neatly into her body.

Tin was already unbuckled and bouncing across the clearing to help remove Khoree's harness.

"Well, well, well, my dragon, what an experience! That was more fun than a trip in a runaway mine cart! You were superb, my friend. That landing was perfect. The launch... Well, maybe we need to work on that. I have to confess it was quite a jolt for us. But, overall, a triumph!"

Khoree looked pleased with herself. She yawned and flexed her full body, her scales rippling impressively.

"The harness is uncomfortable around the wings. And that ice block weighs a lot. I fear this is as far as we can fly today. I must rest. Let me cool my tongue; the flying made it burn."

"Of course, of course. I will adjust the harness accordingly to help around the wings. We have made tremendous progress. I never dreamed we could travel so far and so fast. We must be halfway across the kingdom already! We will be at the Silver Wood in no time at all." While Tin chatted away, he busied himself with ropes and pulleys. A strong tug, and the furs on top of the ice were dragged back. Khoree eagerly snuffled her nose into the opening and flicked her tongue out onto the ice. Tin raised his voice to be heard over the sizzle of cooling dragon tongue.

"There you are, my good dragon. Cold as crystal." Smiling, he turned to Jonah and Summer, who were hanging limply from the safety straps. "And how did you two enjoy the spectacle?"

Jonah had been taking deep breaths, trying to adjust to being on solid ground again. His body seemed to think it was still lurching and swinging wildly beneath the dragon. He fumbled helplessly with the fastenings until Tin came to help.

"I feel like a Frisbee that has been shaken about by a dog," Summer moaned.

"My, my! Really? We don't have that kind of bee here," Tin replied, cheerful as ever.

"Why is the ground still moving?" Jonah managed to say, collapsing onto a fallen log and holding his head in his hands.

"I'm sure that feeling will pass soon enough. I felt much the same way after my first mine cart ride. I'll get some wood for a campfire and we can make ourselves a little feast from the supplies we brought with us. We can rest here for the night and set out again tomorrow morning."

"I think we should be in the Silver Wood by noon," said Khoree, her voice slightly garbled because her tongue was still poking out to lick eagerly at the ice block.

"Wonderful news!" Tin rubbed his hands together in satisfaction. "I haven't spoken with an elf in years."

Lose it all to reach your goal,
At journey's end — your very soul.
Our split desires can come to choke us,
So run with undivided focus.

15

THE SILVER WOOD

"I remember now *why* I haven't spoken with an elf in years!" Tin whispered to Summer, as they panted along behind the strange person who was leading them through the woods. "They spend the whole time looking down their noses at you!"

They were hurrying through a beautiful forest. Khoree had landed in a clearing wide enough to allow for her huge wingspan and the careful setting down of the tongue-tamer. The trees were the largest that Summer had ever seen, some as wide as a house and towering hundreds of metres above their heads. Their trunks were silver-white, and a canopy of bright green leaves filtered the sunlight and cast a dappled shade on the forest floor. It was weak – the sun was shielded by thin clouds – but it was the first time, Summer realized, she had seen any sunshine at all since their arrival in Presadia. It was refreshing and only added to the peacefulness of the forest. The trees here didn't show the same signs of disease that she had seen on her journey to Val-Chasar, or in the mountains as they had climbed to Khoree's cave. Under this peaceful canopy, there was only the faintest wisps of the mist that overwhelmed so much of the kingdom. For the first time, Summer felt she was seeing a glimpse of the kingdom as it might once have been.

Her mind wandered back over the events of the past few days. So much had happened! If only Salt and Antimony could have been here with them too. Their cheeriness and their silly quirks had seemed odd to her at the time, but now she realized how much she missed them. They had bid farewell to each other by Khoree's cave the way you say goodbye to a friend you know you will soon be seeing again. But now, reflecting on the twists and turns of their journey, she wondered when – or if – she would see them next.

Whatever happened, she was determined to learn from Salt's cheerfulness and Antimony's hopeful optimism. They had both wanted to come too, but there had been barely enough room for three as it was, and Tin had left them with plenty to be done in his absence.

Khoree had been leading them, lumbering awkwardly, deep into the woods when Summer noticed, quite by accident, that there were delicate patterns carved into some of the trees. Shortly after she spotted the first of these, an invisible voice broke the peaceful stillness.

"Halt. You are entering into the Silver Wood, home of the elves."

"I know that," Khoree muttered, clearly irritated at the aggressive tone of the hidden speaker. "Greetings, elf. Show yourself. We mean no harm."

Summer hoped Khoree wouldn't lose her temper. Khoree could only carry the heavy tongue-tamer when she was flying so they had had to leave her ice block in the clearing where they had landed.

"It has been many years since dragons and dwarfs entered the Silver Wood," said the invisible voice. "This is a pure place, as yet untouched by the troubles of this dying kingdom–" The voice was cut short by a ragged cough.

"Untouched, is it, elf?" Khoree grunted. "I did not think elves experienced sickness like the mortal races. Perhaps you are not as untouched as you claim. We bring nothing evil into this place that has not already seeped in. We come to speak with your queen on matters of great importance."

A small figure stepped from behind a pale trunk. He looked much like a tree himself: elegant and supple, yet strong. His skin was as pale as the tree trunks and almost translucent, taking on the colours of the forest like a chameleon. He wore a simple linen tunic, which was as green as the leaves. He was hairless, but his scalp was decorated with many small tattoos, which Summer thought looked much like the criss-cross of branches above.

"I will take you to her. But she is not in the habit of entertaining uninvited guests."

"We come in the service of the king. No invite should be necessary," Tin snapped. It was clear to Summer that the dwarf was not impressed by the elf's welcome.

"The king is gone. Queen Ellenair rules Presadia now."

"Does she?" Tin retorted. "If that is true, she does not rule well. The kingdom is in upheaval! Nothing but war, sickness, and chaos. The elves have not bothered with any of the kingdom's affairs in generations. You are not the only one to suffer such a cough, mighty elf." He put a sarcastic emphasis on the word *mighty*. "Many of my dwarfs suffer the same sickness. It is even worse with the humans."

"Silence your uncivil tongue or you shall not see the queen!" said the pale elf with a frown. "We do more than any of the other races to restore this land to its former glory. It was not the elves who corrupted it—"

Tin opened his mouth to argue but Khoree interrupted, her booming rumble drowning out both dwarf and elf.

"Stop your bickering this moment. It seems I am not the only one needing to tame my tongue." Khoree turned to the elf. "Maybe the elves didn't cause the corruption, but they did not hesitate to snatch power for themselves and extend their control over Presadia, only to abandon it when trouble multiplied. Perhaps if your energy had been spent in seeking to restore the king, we would not be in such a mess now. But enough of this. Take us to

Queen Ellenair, or I will stay here and make such a noise that she must come to me."

The elf hesitated for a few moments, casting a distrusting glance at Tin.

"Very well. Follow me. It is not too far."

After ten minutes of attempting to keep pace with their guide, more signs of the elves' settlement became visible. Their forest home was as elegant and simple as the dwarfs' was grand and ostentatious. The trees seemed to stretch taller the further in they went, the roots creating deep, sheltered areas under which awnings fluttered in earthy shades of russet and gold, ochre, and green. In some of these natural hollows, cushions were spread around stone-slab tables where elves reclined, talking in hushed tones, looking up with interest as the unusual party passed by. Some of the spaces looked like workshops, with elves weaving or whittling. Deep under the canopies, Summer could see natural holes, passageways, and spaces beneath the trees themselves, protected from the outside. Lanterns bounced light onto ceilings of pale wood and pillars formed from the very tree roots themselves. As the trees grew larger, the spaces became busier.

As the visitors passed, elves stopped what they were doing to watch the procession, some coming to their doorways and regarding the four strangers with distrust. Summer saw a female elf engrossed in examining a fern whose edges were blackened by disease. Apart from their elf guide's occasional coughing fits, it was the first evidence Summer had seen within the borders of the elf settlement of the decay that was blighting the whole kingdom. With gentle fingers and eyes closed, the elf stroked the leaves. To Summer's amazement, the sickly black marks on the leaf seemed to shrink and were soon banished entirely.

Tin's hushed voice broke the spell.

"Elves have an old magic. They can commune with this natural world. We dwarfs have a natural understanding of stone and metal and jewels. Likewise, the elves have an affinity with all that grows. Just as we shape and craft what comes from the earth with hammer and tongs, so nature responds to them and allows them to shape it." He gave a grudging shrug. "I suppose it is why this corner of the kingdom is less affected by the disease and decay that's getting worse everywhere else.

"Legend has it that when the king ruled, elves were gardeners and stewards of the land. The palace was a sight to behold. It was crafted by the finest dwarf masons, so it goes without saying that it was exceptionally fine, but the gardens too were the most beautiful in all the world."

"It is true," Khoree rumbled behind them. Despite speaking as softly as she could, her words boomed in the peaceful woods, causing several nearby elves to jump. "I remember the palace and gardens well," the dragon went on. "Chiselled stone and living nature, formed in harmony with creation." She gave a wistful sigh.

Leaving the trail between the root-houses, they came over the top of a hill. Beneath them, the ground fell away in an almost perfectly round bowl of soft green grass. The shade of the arching branches overhead gave the vast amphitheatre an enclosed and intimate feel. Hanging from the branches around the space were platforms linked by snaking bridges and ladders. Filled with elves, the amphitheatre would resemble a crowded sports stadium, Summer thought.

In the centre of the bowl-shaped valley was the first stone-built structure Summer had seen in the Silver Wood. A path spiralled around the bowl, letting the visitors appreciate the building.

It was perfectly circular and made of finely cut pure white stone. Slim pillars, like miniature versions of the slender white trees, created a sheltered walkway around the edge. Doors, just visible on the inner side of the walkway, hinted at hidden rooms within. The building was only one storey, but at least three times as high as the elves who strode around the walkway. The top of the building was a large flat disc that doubled as a stage for the amphitheatre. Several staircases gave access to the circular stage. A simple wooden throne sat at the very heart.

They followed the path around and down until they were close enough to be shaded by the building.

"Wait here," the elf instructed shortly.

He turned and walked briskly to the covered walkway before vanishing through one of the inner doors. Summer, Jonah, and Tin sat down on the soft grass; Khoree did her usual arching stretch before settling down to lie like a great dog, her long spine and tail following the curve of the bowl-shaped valley.

"Well! Didn't I tell you elves are rude and proud?" Tin complained.

"Hush, dwarf," Khoree said, not unkindly. "They are our hosts, rude or not."

"I'm wondering if we made the right decision coming here," grumbled Tin, half under his breath.

"Don't say that, Tin." Summer did her best to sound positive. "Everyone agreed the elves were the most likely to know where we should look for the king. They helped him escape. They must know where he went."

"But it was so long ago," pointed out Jonah. "Surely if the queen was meant to marry him, she would have done everything possible to get him back. And anyway, even if they did know then, I'm not sure how much help it will be to us now. It was all so long ago."

"I'm not convinced they'll help us anyway," muttered Tin. "They're only interested in themselves."

"Maybe we should–" Summer started, but was cut off by Tin and Jonah trying to talk over each other.

"Quiet!" Khoree's breath sizzled as she battled her temper. Her shout echoed around the amphitheatre.

Summer, Jonah, and Tin fell silent, their faces sheepish.

"Quiet, little ones," Khoree said again in a softer tone. "We cannot sit here and bicker between ourselves. We have a united purpose. If this doesn't work, then we will think of something else. The elves *may* be proud and rude, but they are some of the oldest servants of the king. We will talk with Queen Ellenair and see what assistance she can offer."

"Hmph, yes. I suppose. Very well," muttered Tin.

After a few moments of awkward silence following Khoree's scolding, Summer asked a question she had been pondering for a while.

"Khoree, you said there was more to the song that Tin sang. How does the rest go?"

"Hmm," said Khoree. "As I said, it is an old song. There are many versions, but the most common goes as follows:

> *Face yourself, what do you see?*
> *Reflected back in honesty,*
> *At once, your pride and vanity,*
> *With visions of what you could be.*

Summer closed her eyes and lay back on the soft grass as the dragon began to sing the now familiar words of the first verse.

Her voice was deep and rumbling, and richer than any human voice. The song welled up from the depths of her vast body and reverberated through it, sending vibrations through the ground, like drum rolls.

> *Live your words and don't just speak;*
> *Protect the poor, defend the weak.*
> *Beliefs are dead when missing deeds;*
> *To speak and do is what we need.*

Tame your tongue and watch your words,
For they have power when said or heard.
They choose your steps and steer your feet,
And reap a harvest, sour or sweet.

Lose it all to reach your goal,
At journey's end — your very soul.
Our split desires can come to choke us,
So run with undivided focus.

Finish as if…

Khoree trailed off, distracted by something on the roof of the building. She lifted herself from her haunches.

"Queen Ellenair," she said, bowing her great head in greeting.

16

THE ELFISH QUEEN

Jonah craned his neck to try to catch a glimpse of the queen, but she was too far back from the building's edge.

At that moment, however, an elf glided silently from the covered walkway before them, gesturing wordlessly for Summer, Jonah, and Tin to follow. Without waiting to see if they would, he turned and headed back to the walkway. Jumping to their feet, they hurried after him. Summer could hear the rumble of Khoree's voice introducing them to the queen.

The elf led them under the shade of the covered walkway. Jonah's eyes widened at its beauty, with its slim pillars and a ceiling that resembled knotted roots. They passed through a narrow door on the inner curving wall. Beyond it was a spiral staircase that emerged onto the flat roof.

Khoree's head and upper body poked up over the edge. In front of her, a small party of elves was gathered on the platform.

The throne was no longer empty. Around it stood four elves, two on each side. Jonah barely saw them. His eyes were drawn to the elf who was sitting on the throne.

Her skin had adjusted to the white throne and was as pale as the moon and flawlessly smooth. She appeared ageless, yet her presence was that of someone with a lifetime of wisdom behind her. Like all the elves she had no hair on her head, only delicate tattoos. To Jonah, this had looked strange on many of the elves, but the elf queen's markings were mesmerizingly beautiful: an array of patterns that flowed from her head and followed the contours of her neck down onto her back.

Unlike the other elves, who wore tunics, she wore a simple and unadorned gown, which pooled on the floor around her feet. Rings, fashioned from the white wood, adorned her fingers. On her head was a circlet of solid gold, around which three strands were intertwined. One strand was of the elfish silver wood, the second was polished iron, and the final jewelled strand glimmered like a dragon's scales.

Jonah stared, awestruck by this vision of elfish loveliness. Tin, emerging on the roof beside him, gasped aloud.

"The crown of the four races," he whispered. "The crown of the true king!"

There was no question that this was Ellenair, queen of the elves. As Jonah, Tin, and Summer emerged from the staircase, she was speaking to Khoree. Her voice, like her appearance, was entrancing: gentle and soothing, yet with a depth that gave it a certainty and authority that made Jonah feel quite nervous. Just as her elfish skin seemed to adopt the colours and shades of the forest, so too her voice seemed layered with the very sounds of nature itself; the breathiness of wind and the musicality of birdsong combined with a strength like that of the ancient trees.

"It has been many years since elves, dragons, dwarfs, and humans all met together in one place. In truth, I had feared that dragons had deserted this land long ago. Pray tell, where have you been for so long?"

"There have never been many of us, even in the days of the king. When he was thrown into exile, this kingdom was no longer a safe place for us. Those who stole the crown – the crown you wear now – desired not just absolute authority and power, but eternal life. All know the power of dragon's blood to extend a mortal's life. After the first dragon was captured and bled dry, the others fled. Where they went, I know not."

"I regret that the elves did not protect you during that dark time. Too many stood by and did nothing."

"And some did more than that," Khoree reminded her.

Queen Ellenair hesitated, a momentary flash of annoyance disturbing the smooth serenity of her face.

"A small number only. I deeply regret the involvement of some elves in the downfall of the king."

"Yet not enough to prevent you wearing that crown," Khoree growled.

The queen contemplated the dragon in silence, her straight back and tilted head proud and unintimidated. After a moment, she broke the tension by turning her attention to the humans and Tin.

"Greetings to you all. Your companion Khoree has told me your names, but not the purpose of your visit. Such an… *unusual* party we have not had in the Silver Wood for as long as I can remember."

Queen Ellenair did not seem concerned about long introductions. It appeared to Jonah as if they were an irritation to the queen. No doubt Tin's bickering with the first elf they had met, and Khoree's jibes at the queen herself, had damaged whatever welcome they were to receive. Fortunately, Summer spoke up before the dwarf or the dragon could offend their host further.

"Queen Ellenair, thank you for your welcome here. It is truly wonderful to see elves and…" Intimidated by the elf queen's formidable beauty and the amused smirk on her lips, Summer was stumbling over her words. "And… we hope you can help us on our quest," she finished lamely.

"Who is this?" asked Ellenair of no one in particular. "A young girl who speaks to an elfish queen before the high lord of all the dwarfs can open his mouth? I assume you are the Summer that Khoree named."

"She is," Tin interjected before Summer could reply, "and she is more than worthy to speak before me whenever she likes. You might be wise to listen to her words yourself. These children have taught me more than I ever believed they could. You do wrong to speak to her with so little respect."

Tin yelped. Summer had trodden on the end of his beard, adding a stern glance for good measure.

"Sorry for the impatience of my friends," Summer continued, ignoring Tin's grumbles.

Jonah flashed Summer an admiring look. It was just as well she was taking the initiative. If Tin and Khoree couldn't be polite, they had no chance of getting help from the elves.

"We have travelled a long way and we are tired," Summer explained. "I am Summer, and this is Jonah, my friend."

Jonah tried to voice something that made sense, but only managed an unintelligible mumble.

"Perhaps your friend was right to correct me," Queen Ellenair replied. "You speak very confidently for one so young, and with more courtesy than your companions." Her eyes roamed across the four travellers. "I will ensure a place is made ready for you to rest in a moment."

She turned to one of the elves standing next to the throne. He nodded and retreated to one of the stairways.

"But before you rest," went on Ellenair, "you must tell me about this quest you mentioned. It must be quite important to enlist the help of a dragon and the high lord of the dwarfs."

"It is," said Summer. "It all started less than a week ago…"

17

KIDNAP

Summer recounted the full story to the elfish queen. She was grateful that Jonah finally got the better of his nerves and spoke up to tell his own parts of the adventure. Even Khoree and Tin seemed to relax. Queen Ellenair listened, her expression unreadable, occasionally asking questions.

"With the mirror destroyed," finished Summer, "there's no way for us to get home. That's why Khoree suggested coming to you."

"To me?" Ellenair raised her eyebrows. "We possess some magic over the natural world but nothing of the kind your mirror had."

"It's not *that* we need help with. Khoree says the mirror was made by the king – that it came from his palace."

At the mention of the king, Ellenair looked away.

"Elves abandoned that place long ago. There is nothing there now, let alone any magic mirrors."

"We know that," Summer persisted. "Khoree believes the only way is to try to find the king and see if he can help."

"Find the king?" As they had recounted their story the queen had grown less frosty, seemingly intrigued by the tale, but at the mention of the king, all her defences snapped back into place and she was once again brusque and cold. "The king is gone. He's either dead or he clearly doesn't intend to return. Ever. I rule now. Your quest will be a fruitless one."

"But you could be our only hope of finding the king and restoring him to the throne."

"I am sorry – we are unable to help you," the queen snapped. "You can go and rest now before you continue your journey."

Summer and Jonah stared at her in disbelief.

Tin, clearing his throat, decided to try.

"Queen Ellenair, the dwarfs are committed to seeing the king found and restored. Why do the elves not join us? Together we could see him rule again…"

"I rule!" Fierce anger blazed in the queen's eyes. "Perhaps the dwarfs should recognize the authority of the elves rather than carving out their own realm. The elves were the most faithful servants of the king. It was the elves who helped the king to escape. It was the elves who overthrew the ones who cast out the king. The elves were the ones who struggled to re-establish order and control when everything went wrong. It is the elves…"

A low vibrating rumble drowned out her words. It shook the building and caused Queen Ellenair's eyes to widen. Like a damn bursting, the rumble became a mighty roar as Khoree towered over the gathered assembly. Opening her tremendous jaws to reveal rank upon rank of viciously sharp teeth, she lifted her head to the sky. A ball of flame exploded above them. Far overhead, leaves shrivelled in the heat, falling as a downpour of ash.

The queen shrieked in dismay and anger.

"Khoree, your temper…" exclaimed Jonah.

"Some anger is good, boy," Khoree thundered. She reared up onto her hind legs, towering high over the building – which suddenly felt inconsequential under the bulk of the armoured dragon. Her shadow fell over the group. Her neck arched over and her fearsome face loomed menacingly above them.

"It is the elves who commit the same wrongs as those first wicked servants! It is the selfish queen who clings to a power not her own – a power stolen from the true king!" Khoree's words were deafening, her hot breath buffeting the group around the throne.

"You claim control over the kingdom. Well, look around you. Look at the land. It dies. Look at the people. They suffer. Look at yourselves. You cling desperately to your power. Your pride prevents you recognizing the mess around you. If you truly were the most faithful servants of the king, you would have done everything possible to see him restored. You would search for him now.

"These children have known of him only a few days and already they are committed to seeing him rule again. You, more than anyone, should desire his return. You, his betrothed. But you can't bear to release your control; you can't bear to surrender the crown you wear so boldly. You claim you are for the king, but you set yourselves up against him."

"How dare you!" the queen practically screamed at Khoree. "I loved the king more than any of you. I sought to protect his kingdom, to look after it until he returned. But he's not coming back! All I long for is to see this kingdom flourish. Do you not think I see the damage? Do you not think I weep at the decay? I can change this. If people would obey me, I could fix this! I have plans. I have–"

"Foolish elf!" Another rush of flame accompanied Khoree's words, its force silencing the proud queen. "Can you not see that your plans have failed? You are unwilling to find the king because you don't want to surrender your power. You don't want to see anyone in charge but yourself."

"This is outrageous!"

"Do you know where the king went into exile?"

The queen hesitated.

"Do you know?" Khoree roared again.

"If the king wanted to return, he would have by now. If he is still alive, he is clearly quite happy to let me rule."

"We waste time," Khoree boomed in frustration. "If you will not help us willingly, then you will help us unwillingly!"

With that she opened her great wings, buffeting them all with a gale force wind that knocked Summer and Jonah over.

Launching from the grassy hill, she clambered up onto the building, which shook and cracked under her as her sharp talons scratched the stone. Before Summer knew what was happening, one huge claw closed around the now cowering queen. She shrieked in rage and fear as Khoree leaped into the air. The vast arena only just gave the dragon room to beat her wings.

Summer looked up to see the dragon filling the amphitheatre, silhouetted by the still-smouldering branches.

She hurtled toward the canopy above and smashed through it, splintering boughs. Leaves and branches, burning twigs and ash showered down onto the grass and building below.

Jonah crashed into Summer, holding his arms up in an attempt to protect them both from the falling wreckage. A moment later Tin did the same, his wiry beard smothering Summer, the small beads pressing cold against her hot face. After a minute or so, the dwarf straightened. Jonah and Summer untangled themselves from their bundle, and looked around them.

The rooftop and grassy bowl were covered in broken branches and charred debris. The remaining elves were craning their necks, staring in bewilderment at the sky. Through the huge hole Khoree had made in the canopy, the dragon could be seen ascending into the sky. In her claw they could just make out the wriggling form of the queen. A moment later, Khoree finished her climb and glided out of view.

A strange silence fell upon the forest. Summer caught the glimpse of movement around the tree line as startled elves emerged on the platforms and the forest floor, looking up in horror.

"Well," Tin's voice seemed to echo around the silent arena, "that was unexpected."

18

THE QUEST TO FIND THE KING

"Why do you think she will have gone back to the clearing?" Jonah asked, panting as they jogged. "She might have just flown off. She was very angry."

Beside him, Summer ducked under a branch in their mad dash.

"Of course she was. That's *why* I know. Her tongue will be hurting after all that fire. You've seen how much she loves the ice and how much it helps with her burning tongue. I bet she's back at the tongue-tamer already, cooling it down."

They continued their rush through the trees, surrounded by an escort of disgruntled elves. Tin had managed to persuade them to take the three of them back to the clearing, explaining that it was all a misunderstanding and that as soon as the dragon had cooled her tongue, she would calm down and they could have their queen back. The elves had been unconvinced, but since they seemed equally unsure of what to do following the kidnapping of their queen, they had agreed and set off quickly through the forest.

Jonah was breathless and sweaty by the time they arrived at the large clearing. Summer had been right. Khoree was indeed there, soothing her tongue on the steaming ice block. Queen Ellenair, looking far less composed and perfect, was pinned beneath her claw and beating her fists uselessly against the armoured foot while protesting loudly. The dragon, distracted by the blissful coolness of the ice, was ignoring her cries.

"Khoree!" Tin shouted with relief. "You must release the queen. It seems these elves are not too happy about what you just did."

Tin, Summer, and Jonah bounded across the clearing, leaving their elfish escort hovering anxiously by the tree line.

The dragon lifted her muzzle from the tongue-tamer.

"No," she said simply.

"What do you mean, no?" Tin spluttered. "You can't just go around stealing queens."

"She will not help us otherwise."

"She's hardly likely to help us now!" Tin replied with exasperation.

"She will," the dragon declared confidently.

"Why?" Jonah asked.

"Because if she doesn't help, I will eat her," Khoree said matter-of-factly, no trace of anger remaining in her voice.

"You'll what?" Summer exclaimed.

"You wouldn't dare!" shrieked Queen Ellenair.

Jonah could hear concerned mutters from the elves in the trees.

"Of course I would," Khoree told them all. "I am a dragon, after all."

"Now now, let's all calm down," Tin said, his voice tinged with desperation. "What if she tells us where she thinks the king might be, and then we let her go?"

"Yes! Yes, I will tell you," agreed the elfish queen eagerly, all shreds of her calm, cool authority gone.

"Where is he?" Jonah pressed.

"We don't know for definite – it was so long ago."

Khoree growled, producing another squeal from the trapped queen.

"I'm telling you," she insisted nervously. "It was long ago, but rumour has it some of our kind helped the king escape from the palace dungeons where his wicked servants had locked him up. Supposedly, they took him to Mount Necros, far to the north, at the very tip of Presadia. It is a cold and inhospitable place. No one would find him there. They thought he would come back soon, but years passed and he didn't. Things just got worse and worse. Then the elves tried to fix things. We took back the crown, tried to restore order—"

"Mount Necros?" Tin interrupted.

"Yes! Yes. Not a nice place, but safe, we thought, from those who would look for him. That's all I know."

"Then to Mount Necros we go," Khoree declared.

"Yes, yes. May I go now?" the queen asked pitifully.

"No," Khoree growled.

"But you said—"

"I said nothing! I'm not letting you out of my sight until we find the king. Who is to say you told us the truth, elf? If he is not there, you will stay with us until we either find where he is, or discover that he cannot be found."

"This is an outrage!" She banged her fist uselessly against the dragon's huge claw.

Jonah noticed that the elves had fanned out and were cautiously approaching the dragon.

"Any closer and I eat her," Khoree rumbled threateningly. The anxious elves stopped, looking uncertainly at each other.

"Now, you have a choice, elf queen. You can get in the tongue-tamer with the others, or stay in my claw, but you are coming either way."

"You can't take me away! I am the ruler. I'm in charge. The kingdom needs me."

"I'll take that as the claw, then."

"No, no, not that again. I'll get in this silly box of yours." Ellenair's voice trembled.

"Right, then. Everyone in. And don't think of trying to run away."

The dragon lifted her paw and poked the elf queen with her nose like a giant dog, pushing her toward the tongue-tamer.

Summer and Jonah jumped in and secured their leather harnesses, shifting how they were positioned to make room for the extra passenger. It was even more of a squeeze than before and Jonah wasn't looking forward to the journey. With a touch of her previous steeliness, Ellenair climbed unceremoniously into the passenger section of the tongue-tamer. She allowed herself to be strapped in by Tin, who had quickly reconnected the required straps to Khoree's harness before squeezing himself into the small amount of remaining space.

Jonah wasn't sure how he felt, being party to the kidnapping of an elfish queen, but Khoree left him little time for moral deliberation as she flapped her wings to hover over the tongue-tamer. Jonah could see the elves crouching, shielding their faces from the buffeting wind as they watched the dragon taking their queen away for the second time that day.

Clasping the specially designed handle of the enormous basket, Khoree swung the tongue-tamer into the air. The clearing shrank beneath them with alarming speed, and Jonah's stomach lurched violently. Beside him Queen Ellenair grasped his arm with a grip so tight it hurt. He didn't know how far Mount Necros was, but he was sure it would be a long journey.

Over the kingdom they flew, alternating between the smooth glides as Khoree rode the rising air currents and the horrible ups and downs as she climbed to ever greater heights. Though the ice had soothed the dragon's temper, she still seemed fuelled by an intense passion. She flew harder and faster than ever. It wasn't until darkness was falling that she set them down for the night.

The day was only just dawning when she woke the group to continue. For three days, they repeated the same cycle of flying and resting. Queen Ellenair remained aloof and unresponsive. Most often she remained silent, refusing to communicate, except to glare at her companions. Khoree forbade her from moving more than a few metres from her. After an attempted escape in the middle of the first night, which ended with Khoree almost burning the terrified elf in her anger, she remained obedient.

As they flew, Jonah became more and more aware of the decay and destruction that had spread through the kingdom. Beneath them, they glimpsed burned villages, abandoned towns, and battlefields filled with ant-sized soldiers.

Much of the land was cloaked in the yellow-tinged mists that seemed to get thicker and more foreboding with every passing day. Even the areas that were free from the mist showed evidence of its passing. Large areas that should have been the greens of grass and trees looked bleached and poisoned. Even far above the land Jonah thought he could smell a damp rotting stench.

At times Khoree would be forced to fly through the bubbling clouds that mirrored the mist below. When she did, the air stung Jonah's face and burned his lungs. The smell, like rotting egg, made him want to gag. Like the mist it seemed to grow thicker each day, producing a sense of evil as it strengthened its grip on Presadia. The dragon complained that the clouds made it hard for her to breathe and Jonah was glad that she sought to fly in the clearer spaces as much as possible. The smell and the clouds both had a deeply threatening presence that filled him with dread.

From above, Jonah could see how the rivers ran sluggish and polluted, dirty brown streaks through a landscape marred with parched and starved plant life. As they continued ever north, they came across a great forest that had been cut down, leaving a desert of stumps. The reason for its fate became visible as they neared the lower-lying mountain range that Khoree told them marked the northern end of the kingdom. Hundreds of ugly furnaces with chimneys that belched plumes of black sooty smoke stretched out in ranks. Lines of workers with bent backs looked up in surprise as the dragon and her cargo flew low over the roofs.

"The workshops of the northern dwarfs," Tin explained, shouting across at Summer and Jonah while shaking his head. "You thought the injustice of Val-Chasar was terrible; I fear these dwarfs have fallen much further. I had heard the rumours, but this is truly horrendous to behold. These people are no free-workers. The dwarfs here cannot even pretend to hold to the king's freedom. Now I see the possible end of the path my dwarfs and I were on, I am even more thankful that you revealed to us the error of our ways."

It was in a subdued mood that they continued their flight, following the edge of the mountain range as it snaked its way to the northern tip of the kingdom.

Some hours later – Jonah found it hard to keep track of time as they flew – they caught sight of an ominous silhouette on the smoggy horizon. To begin with, Jonah assumed it was a darker patch in the cloud, but as they drew closer, he realized it was a mountain of epic proportions. It towered over its brothers and sisters, rising steeply into the sky. It was so tall that the top was invisible, piercing the ceiling of impenetrable poisonous cloud above.

"Mount Necros," said Khoree.

No one replied. There seemed little to say.

On they flew, into the mountain's shadow. Even Khoree, in her gargantuan glory, seemed but a gnat in comparison.

There was a growing weight in Jonah's stomach. The closer they got, the more anxious he felt.

FINISH AS IF CHANGED ALREADY,
PRESSING ON STILL, STRAIGHT AND STEADY,
PERSEVERE FROM BIRTH TO GRAVE,
FOR YOU ARE COUNTED WITH THE BRAVE.

19

MOUNT NECROS

Up and up they flew. The craggy rocks and cliffs of Mount Necros were barren and desolate. Summer sensed an almost conscious malice from the mountain. It scratched away at her conviction. Every wingbeat higher brought with it the increasing desire to shout out that they should stop, turn around, go somewhere – anywhere else but here. All she wanted was to go home. How could the king be in such a place as this? How could a person survive here for so long?

They continued upward. Summer could not imagine how they would have scaled the mountain without Khoree. It seemed an endless and impossible climb with no sign of plants or water. The cliffs and stone bluffs were a black-grey and the rocky earth looked crumbly and dangerous. A savage wind whipped its way around the mountain, causing clouds of fine dust to whirl and eddy in a black blizzard.

"We near the clouds again." Khoree sounded as concerned as Summer felt. "I do not like these clouds. They are unnatural and evil. But we must go up, and there is no break in them. I do not know what we will be able to see, or how far I will be able to go in them. The air is unclean and choking. It stings and I feel it eat away at my insides. You might be wise to cover your mouths and try not to breathe too much."

"What about you?" Summer shouted. She was certain Khoree's voice was hoarser than usual and her breath more ragged as she bellowed back at them through the howling gale.

"Do not fear for me, my girl. Once again, your concern for me warms my heart, but I am merely old and lazy from too many years in a cave."

Khoree was trying to make light of her condition, but Summer wasn't convinced. She watched her friend with concern. Her white talons gleamed less than when they had met, instead looking yellowed and unhealthy. Her glittering blue scales seemed dull and discoloured. They swelled rhythmically as the dragon filled and emptied her huge lungs in the strenuous climb.

Summer imagined breathing in so much of the tainted air and wanted to cry out in protest. Khoree had made up her mind, however, and ever since the dragon had kidnapped Ellenair, Summer had felt a little warier around her friend. Their relationship had grown deep and strong as their quest progressed, but Summer didn't want her affection for the dragon to stop her remembering she was dangerous and sometimes unpredictable.

Tin nudged her and offered her a torn piece of fabric taken from the insulation around the ice block. Smiling her thanks, she accepted it and pressed it to her nose and mouth. It had the same texture as Tin's beard and she wondered if it was made from woven beard hair. It smelled almost like honey and was scratchy against her face but seemed to help as they passed into the poisonous clouds. Jonah had pressed to his face his own ragged shirt. Both he and Summer had been given fresh clothes and fur coats by the dwarfs when they had first set out. It was something Summer had been thankful for, but Jonah had kept hold of his shirt despite its wretched condition, insisting that his mum would be fuming if he lost it.

Summer thought for a moment about her own parents, about

home, about her whole world – which seemed so distant and long ago. She wondered what her parents must be thinking after so long.

Tin offered Ellenair a piece of fabric, and for a moment it looked as if she would ignore him; but with a glance at the unnatural, billowing ceiling of clouds, she swallowed her pride and accepted it.

They soared upward into yellowy smog. It was so dense and smothering that it was like plunging into a bog. Having broken the surface, it was like flying into a storm. The whistling wind below was a light breeze compared to the great gusts that crashed into their huge swinging basket now. The wind stung Summer's eyes, and made her cough despite the fabric covering her mouth and nose. The stinging cloud made her skin itchy and painful. Tin, Jonah, and Ellenair were coughing too and turning their faces away from the tempest, twisting as much as was possible in the leather straps that kept them inside the tongue-tamer. Summer squinted through the smog but could barely see Khoree's body, which was only a stone's throw above them. Her claws, gripping the thick handle of the tongue-tamer, dissolved into the gloom with only hints of the dragon above.

Soon Summer could see almost nothing. All there was was the damp grey-yellow pressing against her from all sides. She closed her eyes, praying for the journey to be over. The tongue-tamer was swinging even more wildly. Khoree was struggling. Through the deafening roar of the wind, Summer heard a louder bellowing as the dragon strained against the strong winds. The bubbling mist above her was lit from within by the ruby red of Khoree breathing fire, revealing for a moment the silhouette of her wings, beating wildly. A moment later it was gone again.

Then, without warning, there was a tremendous smash.

Summer was hurled against the padded furs behind her. An instant later, she was launched forward, only the leather straps saving her from being thrown right out. They dug painfully into her shoulder blades. There was another crash, this time pushing her sideways. Turning her head, she saw a jagged cliff face only an arm's reach to her side. Khoree was still trying to fly and the oversized basket was scraping along the rocky wall like cheese on a grater.

Wood splintered, shreds of fur and bits of the grass insulation spraying in all directions. A sliver of something wet and freezing hit Summer's cheek as the ice block itself smashed along the cliff.

Then, in a moment, the cliff was gone, replaced by cloud once more, with the tongue-tamer swinging out of control.

As they swung violently sideways, Summer heard more wood splintering and felt the vibrations of the ice block sliding. She didn't see it fall free, but the sudden change in weight took the straining dragon by surprise and Khoree twisted above them. Another flash of flame lit the sky, like red lightning illuminating clouds from the inside.

Though Summer could see nothing, she felt the sudden drop in her stomach. Everything seemed to move in slow motion. Looking up, Summer saw that Khoree held the handle with one claw only, her leg twisted awkwardly as she fought to retain her grip.

Then the tongue-tamer hit solid ground. Summer felt herself rolling, head over heels, still strapped tightly beside the others. Miraculously, the wooden frame held together, preventing her and her companions from hitting the ground. After one complete roll, the remains of the contraption slammed to a standstill, its occupants suspended by their straps – staring straight down at the rocky earth beneath them, less than a metre from their faces.

Summer heard a pained roar and crash somewhere in the smog. The mountainside shook with the sounds of a landslide before falling still.

Stunned and exhausted they hung, unmoving.

They were on Mount Necros.

20

KHOREE'S BREATH

Summer fumbled with her leather straps, struggling to release the clasps while they held her full weight. Jonah and Tin had somehow wrestled their way out, and Tin came to help her.

She had to crawl out from beneath the wreckage of the tongue-tamer, which was strewn across the dusty grey earth. Splinters and ripped furs were scattered randomly over the steep slope onto which they had crashed. Summer could see only a stone's throw away before everything melted into the dark mists that cloaked the mountain.

She could hear wracking coughs of a volume that could only belong to Khoree, echoing somewhere on the bleak mountainside.

"How could you do this to me?" Ellenair demanded of no one in particular. "Do you know how unthinkable it is to kill an elf? Dwarfs and humans die so quickly anyway that it hardly matters, but I have lived for thousands of years, only to have a mad dragon almost kill me on a cursed mountain!"

"Stop being so selfish and thinking only of yourself!" snapped Tin, carefully inspecting his beard for damage.

Ellenair looked as if she would answer back, but instead she huffed and turned to walk away from them, picking her way down the dangerous slope. Summer wondered if she intended simply to walk all the way back to the Silver Wood. Maybe, like Summer, she was just overwhelmed by the seriousness of their situation and their close brush with death.

"Should I go after her?" Jonah groaned, rubbing his neck with a pained expression.

"Leave her be. Where can she go?" Tin peered into the fog. "Has anyone seen Khoree?"

Summer shook her head, still stunned from the crash landing. As if on cue, more loud coughs sounded from out of the mist. The echoey mountain and wall of clammy smog made it hard to work out where they were coming from.

"Khoree?" Tin bellowed. "Khoree, where are you?"

Before the dragon could answer, there came the sound of sliding gravel and a tumbling of rocks from below, accompanied by a scream and then a hoarse exclamation from Khoree.

"Be careful, elf!"

"*Me* be careful? It's you, dragon, who hurled us down into this forsaken place! If it wasn't for you..."

Ellenair's words were drowned out by Khoree's coughs.

Summer, Jonah, and Tin made their way in the direction Ellenair had gone.

Summer picked her way slowly and carefully down the slope. It sounded as if Ellenair had triggered a small landslide and Summer didn't want to do the same.

It wasn't too far. Her small field of vision followed her downhill like an orb within the fog, only letting her see the next few steps ahead. She held the piece of material she had somehow kept a hold of to her mouth, thankful for its sweeter smell, which partially masked the stink of rot, and the way in which it lessened the sting of breathing in the toxic air.

After only a couple of dozen metres she saw the evidence of Ellenair's slip. A dozen more and there was Khoree and the elfish queen. Ellenair was half buried under piles of rocks and small stones and was busy scrambling free from the scree, but Khoree lay still, much of her body buried under a crushingly large pile of rocks and stones. Her shoulders and head were clear of the rockslide, her neck convulsing as she coughed. The hillside seemed to shake as the dragon choked on the foul air, her blanket of debris rippling with each attempt to fill her great lungs.

"Khoree! Oh Khoree, are you OK?"

Summer slid down the final stretch to rest her hand on the dragon's neck. Her scales had lost their dazzle and colour. In the gloomy light they seemed almost grey themselves, like everything on this mountain.

"Summer, my girl..." Khoree's voice sounded weak and breathy, as if each word was an effort, "boy, dwarf... my friends. How glad I am you are all right. I am sorry we crashed. I am sorry... sorry I have failed you."

"You have not failed us!" Tears welled in Summer's eyes at the dragon's tone.

Khoree coughed again: painful, uncontrollable coughs. Summer saw her tongue and mouth, blistered and raw from the evil clouds. She imagined her breathing in deep lungfuls of it as she flew them so valiantly up Mount Necros and was horrified at the dragon's sacrifice.

"We would never have got this far without you, dragon," said Tin, trying hard to sound cheerful.

"I cannot... go on." Khoree interrupted herself with another cough. "I fear this is as far as I go with you. These rocks are too great for me to move. They make it hard to breathe.

"You must continue on in search of the king. I grieve that I will not see him again. I wish I could have said... I wanted to tell him how sorry I am." She paused, breathing deeply as if catching her breath. "Sorry that I turned my back on him all those years ago, sorry that I let my tongue rule me, let my anger keep me away from him. I hoped I would see him one more time..."

Summer, tears streaming down her face, gulped down a sob.

"Khoree, stop speaking like this. You will be fine. You are a dragon. Dragons don't die! You *will* see him."

"Perhaps not from old age or common illness, but these clouds that choke the kingdom are no natural thing. I have breathed them long and deep in the flight." Khoree coughed again. "Do not be sad for me. I have lived for millennia. Too much of that time I have grumbled and complained. I feared suffering so much that I allowed my anger and misery to keep me huddled in a cave, hiding in shame. I have lived more life in the last week than in centuries before that.

"Life without purpose is meaningless, and there is no better purpose than the purpose for which we were designed. I was born to serve the king. For too long I have denied that. For too long I thought I was unworthy. But that is my life's purpose. It is better that my life should end here, fulfilling that purpose, than to live forever, ignoring it." Khoree's breath was wheezy and her words gruff and quiet. Her eyes looked at them each in turn with affection and woe, and yet in their depths was a deep peace.

"One breath in the service of the king is worth more than a lifetime of breaths in service to ourselves. One wingbeat toward my king is worth more than any other journey. One opportunity to help in seeing his kingdom restored is worth more than anything and everything else I have ever had."

"Don't leave us, Khoree." Summer, sobbing now, wrapped her arms around the dragon's neck, pressing her face to the rough scales. It was like trying to cling to a mighty tree; she felt the strange texture so clearly against her tear-stained cheeks. The scales were losing their warmth, the cold of the mountainside penetrating the struggling dragon's inner fire.

"You will be fine, girl. Continue on. Find him. See him back on the throne again. He can help you return to your home; I know it, deep in my bones."

Behind Summer, Jonah was crying too. For a long moment, Summer stayed where she was, pressing her cheek into Khoree's scales, feeling the ragged breaths and letting her tears trickle onto the dragon's neck.

She felt a light touch on her arm and turned to see Tin's grave face. "Come. Khoree is right. We should press on."

"B-but… we don't know where we are going," Summer blubbed.

"Maybe we don't know our exact destination, or the exact route, but we know the direction. Upward, always upward, no matter how difficult and no matter what the cost. All we can do is take the next step and make sure it's heading in the right direction. If we keep doing that, we will eventually get to the right place."

Turning, he trudged slowly back up the slope.

With a final look at Khoree, Jonah turned and followed, still sniffing and wiping tears from his face with his sleeve. Behind Summer, Khoree stirred. Very softly she started to sing.

> *Finish as if changed already,*
> *Pressing on still, straight and steady,*
> *Persevere from birth to grave,*
> *For you are counted with the brave.*

It was the final verse. Summer stood, letting the dragon's voice fill her. It was as if the music flowed into her soul as quickly as the tears poured down her filthy face. When she had finished, Khoree let out a deep sigh as people do when arriving home after a long and difficult journey. Summer waited for the next breath, but Mount Necros was unbearably silent.

After a long pause, there was a crunch as Tin and then Jonah wordlessly restarted their climb.

With the dragon's song still in her heart, Summer turned to follow.

As she did, she saw Ellenair standing a small distance away. She was staring wide eyed at the dragon, her face stricken. She caught Summer watching and, for a moment, she looked as vulnerable as Summer felt. Without speaking, she turned and set off back up toward the crash site.

21

THE CHASM

They had scavenged the crash site for anything useful. Only a few of their supplies had survived, and it was with desperately little that they had turned their backs on the ruined tongue-tamer and begun to climb.

Jonah had been surprised when Ellenair returned to the crash site and joined them in the search for salvage. Tin and Summer had accepted her presence without comment, so Jonah said nothing, wondering if she would head off again in the opposite direction. If she were to do that, Jonah didn't think anyone would stop her – not now Khoree was gone. Khoree had been the one who had kidnapped her. From what Jonah had seen, the elf queen was proud, cold, and desperate to leave them.

She surprised him further, therefore, when she started to climb with them. Tin nodded to her but said nothing.

They climbed in silence. Navigating the loose rocks absorbed all their attention and Jonah kept his head down, focusing on each step before him. Looking up served little purpose since the smog hung thick about them. He held his ruined shirt to his mouth, wishing he could likewise cover his stinging eyes. As they climbed, the fog got darker and Jonah realized it must be nearing night-time.

Up and up they trudged, always climbing. They walked until

Jonah felt he would collapse from exhaustion. He and Summer were beginning to trail quite far behind the surprisingly hardy elf and stocky dwarf. Eventually, loose stones and dirt gave way to sheer rock. Tin called a halt to their climb and, pressing up close to each other, they sat with their backs to a large boulder that offered some small shelter. Curling their legs to try and escape the howling wind, they huddled together miserably. They spoke very little. The events of the day were too overwhelming to discuss yet, and their bodies and minds were too tired from the physical difficulties of the journey.

Ellenair sat down with them – the first time she had chosen to stay so close. Her elfish skin had taken on the greys of the mountain, giving her a hollow and aged appearance and making her dark tattoos appear more like streaks of dirt and dust. She looked dishevelled and lowly in her soiled gown. But, more than appearance, the layers of pride and condescension had been stripped away, leaving something that, to Jonah, was far more beautiful than the perfect queen on her ivory throne.

Jonah noticed that clenched in her hands was the beautiful crown that she had been wearing when Khoree took her. She clung to it like a lifeline, the fierceness of her grip turning her pale knuckles white.

She saw Jonah looking.

"It is beautiful, is it not? The four-stranded crown, the symbol of the four races." Her voice was quiet and stripped of its usual hardness. She ran her fingers along the distinct strands as she spoke. "Gold for the dwarfs, iron for humankind, gemstones for the dragons…" She paused for a moment. Jonah was sure they were all thinking of their friend. "… And silver wood for the elves; all woven together in harmony. The best of all races, brought together in the king." Jonah watched Ellenair caressing the crown. She seemed to be talking to herself, staring at the circlet but seeming to look beyond it.

Jonah waited for her to continue, but she remained silent, caught up in her thoughts and memories. He shuffled himself to try and get comfortable on the lumpy rocks and closed his eyes.

He dozed, despite the aches and pains that seemed to have invaded his whole body. He wasn't sure how long he had fluttered in and out of sleep, but he was properly awake when Tin coughed: a harsh, grating sound. The dwarf heaved himself up and stretched his short stiff body, gathering up his beard, which he had spread over the four of them like a blanket, and carefully wrapping it around his neck again. Jonah felt comforted by the ritual, which Tin performed every morning, of looking after his beard with the utmost care. Even here, on a barren mountainside, cloaked in sooty clouds, and heartsick for their lost friend, he still groomed and handled his beard as if it were a priceless artefact.

"It's still dark," Jonah groaned, realizing how cold he had become, but unwilling to stand up and leave the shelter of their rock and the warmth of Summer beside him.

"It is," the dwarf agreed, "but we have been here many hours. It only seems to be getting darker, though night should have passed long ago…"

"I fear the kingdom will only grow darker from this point onward," said Ellenair, sounding more together than the previous evening. "The journey here…" She paused, shaking her head in dismay. "This kingdom is in far worse condition than I ever thought. It truly is dying." There was a quiet desperation in her voice, as if she were admitting the truth to herself for the very first time.

"Is that why you stayed with us?" asked Summer.

Ellenair thought for a moment.

"Yes," she admitted, "in part. I had not wanted to allow myself to believe things were this bad. I always thought I could fix it all, or keep the darkness back, the way we have at the Silver Wood. With our magic, we can restore some of creation to how it should be. But there is too much sickness in this land. We can treat some of the symptoms but we don't have a cure. This terrible mist is a sign of the end. If I were to return home now… well, I don't think it would be worth returning, knowing the darkness and evil that crouches at our doorway."

"You speak the truth," said Tin.

"But what really changed everything was your dragon's sacrifice. She… she should have lived forever, yet she was content to lay down her life for this cause. That is no small thing for a dragon."

Jonah thought about Khoree. Had she known the journey would cost her so much? He certainly hadn't dreamed that he would end up where he was. All they had wanted was to get home, but this search for the king had taken on a greater importance. Khoree had been willing to give her life to see the king returned to his throne. She had valued that even more than her own long life.

"Come," said Tin, tightening the straps that held the axe to his back, "I know it is the last thing our aching joints want, but we should press on. This horrid fog means we have no idea how far we have to go, and we have precious little to sustain us, which means time is of the essence."

Tin's cheery enthusiasm in the face of their gloomy circumstances amazed Jonah. It spurred the exhausted party to begin the wearying climb again. Jonah's stomach rumbled terribly, but he knew how little food they had salvaged from the wreckage and trudged onward, determined not to think of roast dinners and cooked breakfasts.

They walked – as far as they could tell in the perpetual yellowy dusk of the cloud – most of the day, stopping occasionally to rest. Every now and again they would eat a tiny amount of their dwindling supplies, or take a sip from Tin's leather flask, their only source of water. All of them were coughing now. The effort of climbing meant they couldn't easily keep their noses and mouths covered.

Jonah resorted to trying not to breathe too deeply. The air felt rough and foul in his mouth and left blisters on the insides of his cheeks and throat.

Almost without warning, the party emerged from the smog. It was like surfacing from a great lake. Mount Necros – an island cut off from the world below and surrounded by a bubbling ocean of yellowy fog that stretched as far as the eye could see – rose up before them. Jonah breathed deeply for the first time in what felt like forever. Although the air was now clear of the yellow cloud it was still dim; a cold twilight with no sign of the sun. The strewn boulders and jagged surface of the mountain prevented them seeing clearly how much further they had to go, but higher up Jonah could see huge flocks of birds swirling in endlessly transforming patterns. They filled the sky above, as thick as the clouds below. His short-lived relief died within him as he considered climbing through the chaotic swirl.

The air was icy cold, and after the clamminess and stench of the fog, it seemed strangely dry and dead. The frosty air did, however, offer some small relief for his red itchy skin.

They restarted their climb, hoping to put some distance between them and the hated mist that had so tormented them before resting again. Small moth-like creatures fluttered irritatingly around them. Soon there were clouds of the things as well as other insects that buzzed incessantly, dopily flying into him or landing on the thick fur coat he wore. Jonah realized with dread that the eddying black flocks he had seen were not just birds, but great swarms of moths and insects.

"I think they have fled the mists," Ellenair commented. She seemed less bothered by the insects than the dwarf or the humans, but her grave expression showed concern. "They are not evil, but they have been driven here by what is happening below."

They may not have been evil, but it was extremely unpleasant and Jonah found himself flapping constantly as he tried swatting them. Insects were all very well to look at under a magnifying glass in the corner of the playground, but this was horrible. His flapping proved useless, however, and eventually he resigned himself to putting up with them as they landed on him and flew around his face. Where possible the party tried to avoid the thick swarms, but sometimes they were forced to pass right through the middle, and Jonah resorted to burying his mouth and nose in the collar of his coat and squinting, climbing as quickly as he could to get out the other side. He began wondering if the poisonous cloud might be preferable to all these creepy-crawlies.

The only relief that day was that the wind died down, leaving the mountain still and quiet, though the hard climb made Jonah warm enough that he soon regretted its absence, despite the chill air. As they climbed, the breeze dropped entirely, leaving the air feeling heavy and stale.

The landscape changed, always ascending steeply, ever more treacherous. Often the ground was so steep that all four of them were forced to crawl up, placing each foot and hand carefully so as not to slide back down. At the top of one such section was a flat area, in front of which a huge chasm dropped into invisible darkness below them. The opposite side was a rough steep slope, much like the one they had been climbing. The cliff that dropped away immediately beneath them, on the other hand, was smooth and far too steep to climb down.

"What are we supposed to do now?" said Summer, her voice wobbly with despair and exhaustion.

Jonah picked up a rock and dropped it over the edge. He counted to four before he heard a distant crack and rattle as the rock hit the bottom.

"That's a long way down," he said anxiously, swatting at a particularly annoying moth.

"It is," Tin agreed, frowning. "I can't see any of us getting down there without a rope. If only we had some!" He sighed. "Well, if we can't climb down it, we will have to see if we can go around it."

"But which way do we go?" Jonah looked left and right. The chasm zigzagged out of sight in either direction, like a great wound in the mountain's side.

"Why don't we split up?" Summer suggested. "Two of us go one way and the other two go the other way."

Jonah looked at his friend in admiration. Summer constantly surprised him with her bravery. The brooding mountain was scary, and the thought of splitting up made it even worse.

"What if we get lost? I'm sure it's getting even darker," he ventured.

"We can't get lost if we stick to the cliff edge and only walk a certain distance then come back. If we find something, then we come back here."

"An excellent idea!" Tin agreed with his customary cheerfulness. "If we count our paces and follow the cliff, we'll all know how to get back. Ellenair and Summer, you head left for five hundred paces, and Jonah and I will head right for five hundred. After that, we turn around and come back, even if we haven't found anything."

Reluctantly, Jonah followed the dwarf, still brushing at the flies and moths that insisted on landing on him. Tin hummed lightly and the bright little tune seemed to hold the growing darkness at bay.

22

The Dwarf's Treasure

"Four hundred and ninety-eight. Four hundred and ninety-nine. Five hundred."

Tin halted in front of Jonah.

"Nothing," Jonah said sadly, craning to peer further ahead on the off-chance there was something just beyond. "There hasn't been a single place to cross." He threw another stone down into the chasm, counting to six before the clatter echoed back.

"It's even deeper," Tin said with a sigh. "Well. Maybe Summer and Ellenair fared better in the other direction. Let's head back and see."

It was an effort for Jonah to drag himself back, again counting the steps in his head while Tin counted out loud in a valiant attempt at a heartening mining chant.

Ellenair and Summer were already back when Jonah and Tin neared the starting point.

"Any luck?" called out Summer as they emerged from a particularly thick cloud of insects.

Jonah shook his head. "No. You?"

She shook her head too and Jonah's hope vanished. "What do we do now?" Summer sank down wearily onto the hard ground.

"What can we do?" Jonah shrugged his shoulders in resignation.

"We'll just have to go back. Without rope we'll never get down there. Maybe we missed some near the crash site."

Tin shook his head. "There wasn't any," he said with certainty. "The only things that might have helped was the straps I made for Khoree's harness, but I think they must have been buried with…" He cut his sentence short, sitting down on a nearby rock with a sigh.

They sat in hopeless silence for a moment.

"Well," Tin said eventually, and even he sounded weary now. "We should get some rest. Whatever we do, it can wait until we have all slept."

Jonah didn't need to be told twice. His body was so tired that every fibre of his being was crying out for it. Arranging himself to be as comfortable as possible on the hard stone, he let his body drag him into sleep, too tired to even care about the ever-present moths and insects that crawled over his face. The last thing he saw was Tin, sad and thoughtful as he sat stroking his beard. Then he was asleep.

He awoke to the all-too-familiar sound of coughing, echoing Tin's ragged barks with his own. They might have left the fog below, but his throat and mouth were still painful. He stretched, dragging his heavy eyelids open to stare at the gloomy mountainside. Rolling over, he looked at their makeshift camp, at the huddled forms of Ellenair and Summer, still sleeping close beside him, and Tin, awake and alert, a little way away, working away feverishly at something Jonah couldn't quite make out.

He sat up abruptly, blinking sleep from his eyes.

"Tin, your beard! You…"

Tin glanced up from his work. His eyes were filled with tears.

His glorious beard, his pride and joy, the source of his authority, was chopped off only a finger's width beneath his chin. The crazed shape of what was left would have been comical had Jonah not known the depth of connection and importance that Tin's beard had held for him. The glorious beard lay beside him, piled up like a small hairy mountain, its silvery magnificence dulled now it was disconnected from his chin.

He was plaiting a length of rope from the pile of hair. Already there was quite a length coiled on the ground in front of him.

Tin dropped his eyes to his work again, his nimble fingers plaiting deftly.

The others were awake now, startled by Jonah's exclamation. Summer sat up beside him with a cry of dismay as she saw the dwarf's roughly shaven face.

"You've cut off your beard!"

"Yes…" muttered Tin. "Yes. Well, we needed rope. It was the only way…"

"Oh, Tin!" Summer scrambled to her feet. Rushing over to the dwarf, she threw her arms around him. "Your beard meant everything to you, though!"

"It did," he agreed sadly, "but I have come to realize it is not everything."

"But I thought the only reason you are high lord is because you have the longest beard?"

"It is. It was. By cutting it off, I have forfeited that honour and all that goes with it." The dwarf took a deep breath. "No longer do I live in a palace and own fine things. No longer am I high lord. I am but a dwarf. It's strange to say it, for my wealth has always been the most important thing, but… well… it seems less important here. We need rope if we are to get down this chasm and find the king."

"I don't think I have ever seen a more lordly dwarf, Tin of Val-Chasar." Ellenair drew herself up to her full height and her words resounded with a strength Jonah had not heard from her since she sat on her throne in the Silver Wood.

"What is wealth here?" Tin looked up at her and forced a smile. "These pesky moths have eaten my fine clothes, that terrible fog corroded the metal of my armour and axe. Even before that, each night as I tried to sleep, I remembered the people who were exploited and used to gain our wealth. My wealth is nothing to me now. I would rather lose it all here and be beardless and penniless, knowing I have done all I can to see the king back on his throne."

He coughed painfully, his tuft of rough-hewn beard making him look pitiful and smaller than ever.

"You may not have your wealth now, dwarf," Ellenair told him, "but you have something of far greater worth. I see in you something that has been lost for too long. It's the spirit of Presadia. It is how the legends speak of those who served the king, truly and wholly, when he reigned. You are richer now than you have ever been."

Tin blinked the tears from his eyes. Summer hugged him again while Jonah smiled at the dwarf with fresh respect.

Tin went back to his plaiting, only this time they could hear him humming a little tune.

It took Tin a full day to finish his rope. He insisted on doing it alone. Watching the skill with which Tin's clever fingers worked, Jonah was sure he would not have been able to do it half as well anyway.

Finally, Tin straightened his back and held up his rope with a mixture of pride and sadness.

"This should be more than long enough," he said. "Let's try it."

Looping the end around a jutting rock, he secured the rope with a sturdy knot before dropping it over the edge. It unlooped lazily as it dropped from sight. A quiet thump echoed and the rope pulled tight. Tin smiled proudly.

"Seems like it's done the job," he said, a touch of his old cheeriness back in his voice. "So, who wants to go first?"

Jonah shuffled his feet. He wasn't sure he wanted to go down into the dark chasm on his own and wait all alone at the bottom for the others. Fortunately, Ellenair saved him.

"I can go. I am used to climbing. Our trees are as smooth as this rock, though I must confess, our ropes are nowhere near as fine as this. Truly, dwarf, you have woven a masterpiece."

Tin nodded at the compliment, and with no more fuss, Ellenair slid over the cliff edge, using the rope to abseil down gracefully. Jonah was sure she made it look a whole lot easier than it was.

"Here, one of you take the water." Tin passed the leather flask to Summer. "And this. It's all the food that's left." He handed the small provisions bag to Jonah.

"Why are you giving it to us?" Summer asked, confused.

"Someone has to stay up here and undo the rope for you. You might need it again before you reach the top of the mountain."

"Tin, no!" exclaimed Jonah at the same time as Summer cried, "You can't!"

"I can... and must. What if you come across another place where you need rope? It won't be much good if it's hanging here. You go down and I can untie it and throw it down to you."

"But you will be stuck here all alone!" argued Jonah. "Why does it have to be you?"

"You are the ones who need to get home. I've helped get you this far. I'm not going to let you stop now. No, don't argue with me. It's the way it must be. You must find the king. Do it for me."

"But, Tin—" said Summer.

"I'll be all right," he interrupted her, with the gruff cheeriness they had come to love. "You can always collect me on your way back."

He pulled them both into a firm hug, his stubby beard brushing their foreheads.

"It has been an honour being your friend. You opened my eyes to so much. For that I am eternally thankful."

"Tin, you have been amazing," Jonah mumbled into the dwarf's shoulder. "We will see you again. I know it."

"I'm sure you will." Tin's voice sounded gruffer than ever. "And you'll bring the king with you – I am sure of it. Now hurry along. Ellenair will be waiting for you and time wasted is time lost."

With a lump in his throat, Jonah stepped back toward the edge of the cliff. Tin smiled and raised his hand in a final farewell as Jonah gripped the rope with both hands and, remembering how Ellenair had done it, let himself carefully down the sheer rock face.

He was so thirsty, he was surprised at the tears trickling down his face. As he inched his way down the cliff into the darkness below, he heard the dwarf raise his hearty voice, singing the now familiar song.

23

THE CROWNLESS QUEEN

The climb down was far harder than Ellenair had made it look. The rope burned Jonah's hands, and all his muscles were on fire by the time he reached the bottom, bruised and scraped from his encounters with the cliff. When Summer dropped the final few metres a couple of minutes later, she was in much the same condition, trembling and exhausted.

A moment later, the rope started to wiggle as though alive, then dropped into a heap, the end smacking the ground with a thump.

"The dwarf remains above?" asked Ellenair. She didn't look surprised.

Summer nodded, fighting to keep the tears from spilling over.

Ellenair stared upward, then she gave a little nod. "Then we press onward. It cannot be too much further."

They had to make their way along the chasm some way before they found a part of the slope that would be easy enough to climb. They resumed their pattern of walking, climbing, and resting. Soon, all their food and water was gone. The darkness was growing deeper, though Jonah was sure it must be daytime.

The slope had been getting steeper. They were now climbing a near vertical wall. It didn't help that the rocks jutting out from the face of the cliff were not always secure. Summer had to test each one before putting too much weight on it. Even then some dropped away from under her, and her heart would lurch as she desperately grappled for another hold. Jonah was ahead of her, Tin's rope around his waist as he shifted awkwardly from one hold to another, climbing upward like a clumsy spider.

Summer paused to look down. Ellenair was bringing up the rear a few metres beneath her. Her tattooed head was slick with sweat and her gown that had once been so beautiful was torn and filthy, and full of moth holes. Since she had no pocket or bag, she carried the elegant crown around her upper arm, where it bobbed and jiggled as she climbed. She looked up and saw Summer watching her.

"You are doing well," she said to Summer with a rare smile. "Keep going!"

Scrambling up as best she could, despite the complaints of her muscles, Summer felt as if she had been climbing forever. Every tug on her weary arms made her feel as if the last ounce of her strength was being drained from her. It was a huge relief when she finally saw Jonah clambering over a ledge above her. At last, a chance to rest!

A shower of stones and earth rained down over her as the edge of the ledge crumbled under Jonah. She pressed herself into the cliff, her eyes squeezed tightly shut until the miniature landslide ceased. Daring once again to open her eyes and look up, she saw that Jonah had managed to gain the safety of the ledge.

"I'm at the top!" he called down to them. "Be careful, it's crumbly."

It was crumbly. As Summer hauled herself up, she felt the edge give way under her. Jonah grabbed her arms and pulled, and then she was there, face down on the ground and panting in exhaustion.

"Come on." Jonah prodded her. "Let's give Ellenair a hand."

With a groan, Summer crawled with him to the cliff edge, the two of them inching forward on their bellies as carefully as possible on the unstable ground.

Ellenair was almost at the top. Leaning out, Jonah and Summer gripped her arms to help heave her onto the ledge.

The ground shifted. Summer felt a dizzying sensation as the cliff edge broke away beneath her, rocks and earth tumbling down the cliff face.

With a shriek of alarm, Ellenair slid backwards beneath the cascade of earth and stone.

Summer and Jonah clutched tighter, but their hands slipped on Ellenair's smooth, silky skin. In desperation, Summer let go of the elf's arm and grabbed instead at the delicate crown. Ellenair's arm slipped through. Her eyes were wide and panicked, staring up at Summer in horror. At the last moment, her fingers caught hold of the circlet.

"Jonah! The crown! Quick!" shouted Summer through gritted teeth. "She's too heavy for me!"

Jonah grabbed the crown, and they clung on for dear life. The unstable ground settled beneath them. Summer panted through clenched teeth, her fingers feeling as if they were about to be pulled from their sockets.

Ellenair's feet scrambled at the cliff, searching desperately for a foothold. Loose stone and crumbly black earth showered down beneath her.

"Stop!" Jonah shouted at her. "You'll make the cliff edge give way!"

Ellenair stopped scrabbling, looking up with fear-filled eyes.

"Jonah," Summer whispered, the strain of trying to hold the queen making it hard to speak. "I can't hold her much longer. She's too heavy."

"Hold on. There must be a way to save her."

"No." Ellenair's voice sounded afraid but it rang with the same authority it had had on their first meeting. "No. Trying to save me will only cause us all to fall. I have clung to this crown my whole life. I turned my back on the king. I knew he must be out there somewhere, but I wanted to rule. I didn't want to surrender my power."

"I'm slipping," Summer hissed at Jonah. She closed her eyes, willing every ounce of strength into her grip.

"If... if you find the king," Ellenair begged, "give him the crown. It is his. I only wish I had been able to surrender it in person."

Summer's fingers were slipping. Then, in a moment, the strain was gone. Snapping her eyes open, she stared with horror at the crown, still clasped in their hands. Beyond it there was nothing but the cliff, dropping away into the darkness.

"Ellenair!" Jonah gasped beside her.

Numb with shock, they lay unmoving. Their friends were all gone: Khoree and Tin, who had done so much to help them; and now Ellenair, the once proud elf whose cold manner had warmed and softened as their journey went on, and whom they had grown to respect and care for.

They were alone.

24

MIRROR MOUNTAIN

Ever on and ever up, Jonah marched through the deepening darkness. His body, somehow, put one foot in front of the other, despite the aching weariness that had wormed its way into his bones, and the constant coughing that made his chest hurt and his throat sore.

The clouds of flying insects had dissipated, thankfully, but their absence made the mountainside feel even more lifeless and depressing. He no longer bothered to lift his head as he walked. Instead, he stared only at his feet, crunching relentlessly over the black earth.

In his left hand, he carried the four-stranded crown.

His eyes burned. He was sure that tears would have welled had he not been so thirsty, and had he not shed so many since arriving on Mount Necros.

It was like a nightmare, trying to get somewhere but never reaching it, no matter how long he kept going.

Why were they still climbing?

There had been nothing but sadness on this terrible mountain. Why press on? Why keep going? The journey had cost them everything, and for what? The vague possibility of finding a long-lost king; the slightest rumour that he might have come this way centuries before.

How stupid could they be? Anyone with half a brain would have told them how foolish they were to keep going.

But what else could they do? Go back?

Jonah's feet kept on.

Left.

Right.

Left.

Right.

There had to be a king. There just had to be!

"Please! Please be there," he murmured under his breath.

On he walked, still coughing.

Left.

Right.

Left.

The black earth crunched under his boots, like ash.

Left.

Right.

Something glittered in the blackness. Jonah's steps faltered.

"Jonah... what is it? Do you need to rest?"

"I saw something," he told Summer. "On the ground."

He nudged the earth with his boot, revealing a sparkling shard of glittering crystal the size of his little finger.

"What is it?" Summer stooped to pick it up. "It's beautiful," she said, turning it over in her hands.

Even in the near darkness, the bright fragment seemed to reflect what little light there was. As Summer held it up, a flash of rainbow brilliance shone out across the bleak mountainside.

Summer gave a low chuckle, broken by another fit of coughing.

"It's so beautiful. I miss the colours, and life and... and... everything. I'm so sick of grey and black, and dust and cloud."

Jonah said nothing.

"Do you think we will ever get home, Jonah?"

He looked up at her and the light from the shard showed him how filthy she was, covered in the dirt and grime of the mountain. Smudged tear streaks had left patches of lighter grey over her cheeks. Her hair was all over the place and she looked half wild.

He met her eye but said nothing.

"Do you think he's even there?"

Still he didn't answer.

"Is it worth it?"

"Yes," he said at last. "It has to be. Khoree, Tin, Ellenair, they all gave so much because they believed in the king. I know it feels like it's too hard, and it's cost too much, and it can't possibly be worth it, but something tells me we *must* keep going. For their sakes. So that they weren't left behind for nothing."

"You're right." Summer nodded and lifted her head. "We need to find this king. We need to keep going."

She looked back at the small mirror shard, holding it out so Jonah could see it too. The occasional flashes of colour as the dim light refracted in the mirrored surface were like flashes of memory. Jonah felt almost as if he could glimpse the beautiful kingdom, no longer covered in gloom, but shining with life and colour. He caught glimpses of their own reflections too, and it seemed to him they were almost unrecognizable from the people they had been when they stumbled into Presadia. It felt like so long ago.

A breeze tickled his cheek, the first time the air had stirred in a long time. Its light touch was refreshing and roused Jonah from his trance-like stillness.

"Come on," he said.

Right.

Left.

Right.

Left.

There were more crystal shards now, glinting in the black, sooty dust. The flashes of brightness, along with the breeze, breathed an injection of energy into his joints and muscles.

The longer they walked, the more shards there were glimmering in the earth. Some were quite large, easily the size of Jonah's forearm.

"Jonah, look!" Summer gasped.

Looking up, Jonah saw that they had reached a small ridge. From here, they could see the final ascent. For the first time they could see the mountain peak. He stared open mouthed.

Piercing right through the skin of the mountain, huge towering shards of mirrored crystal, like pillars of dazzling glass or shining church spires, soared skyward, ringing the mountaintop with a spikey crown that shone with brilliance even in the near darkness.

"It's beautiful!" breathed Summer.

Jonah had to agree with her. After all the darkness and dust, and gloom and sadness, the glittering towers were breathtakingly beautiful.

"Come on!" he urged, his voice barely a croak. "We'll rest under that big one over there."

Their motivation carried them to the edge of the mountain's crown speedily. They wove their way through the sparse forest of sparkling glass toward a large shard that rose higher than the others. Once inside the ring of crystals, it took far longer than Jonah had expected. Their path wound backward and forward between the pillars, which grew bigger and taller the further they walked.

He stared in awe at the spikes, marvelling at the rainbow colours, and catching flashes of their reflections bouncing in strange angles and directions. He was certain he saw flashes of other people and places out of the corner of his eye, but when he looked closer, they vanished. He blinked and shook his head, trying to wake himself up.

"I never imagined I could feel this tired," he said to Summer. "My head is playing tricks on me."

"Mine too," said Summer. "Just now, I was sure I saw Khoree over there, but when I looked it was just our reflections."

"I thought I saw those ugly factories we flew over. I think we are so tired we're almost dreaming."

Summer frowned. "I'm not sure. They seem too vivid to be dreams. Do you think these are like the mirror we came through? You know – the way it showed more than a normal mirror would, or… I'm not sure, but I don't think it's just us being tired."

Jonah looked around again, concentrating on the flickering colours and images at the very edges of his vision. It was frustrating. Every time he thought he saw something, it would disappear again. He was sure he caught a glimpse of a forest of dead trees, a village burning, crowds of frightened people dressed in rags. But the images instantly dissolved and all he could see was his own weary reflection and the flashes of rainbow colour.

"Come on," he said. "Let's keep going. We're almost there."

"I can't." Summer leaned heavily on a mirrored rock twice her height. She looked ready to fall over.

"You can. Come on, Summer, try. It's not much further."

"But my feet are so heavy. I'm just… I'm so tired. Please, let's rest here."

Jonah hesitated. It was so tempting just to stop and lie down. To let himself fall asleep. Yet if he did that, he knew he would never get up again. They had no more food or water. His tummy ached with hunger; his tongue was like rough wood in his dry mouth; every inch of his body hurt. Maybe they should just lie down here and forget it all. It would be so much easier.

"No." His own firmness surprised him. "We can do it. *You* can do it. Let's lean on each other. It will be easier that way. See, it's not too far. We can make it."

25

PRESADIA FALLEN

It didn't feel much easier leaning on Jonah. Summer felt as if she was dragging a huge weight behind her. It was as if the ground was clutching at her legs, trying to pull her down. But Jonah pulled her on, toward the big shard.

"It's not getting any closer," she complained, after they had hobbled what felt like another mile.

Jonah's cough was getting worse, horrible to listen to. Oh, for a glass of cold water to wet her mouth and soothe her throat!

Step by painful step they crept toward their destination.

Finally, with only twenty or thirty metres to go, Summer's legs buckled underneath her. She dropped to the ground, dragging the equally tired Jonah down too.

They lay still, trying to catch their breath. Summer waited for Jonah to urge them on again.

He didn't.

Summer turned her head, looking at her friend. His eyes were shut, and he was panting.

"Jonah."

He didn't respond, but she could see his chest moving with his quick, shallow breaths.

"Jonah!" she tried again, louder.

He stirred, opening his eyes drowsily and turning his head to look at her.

"I'm done," he said.

Summer wanted to crawl to him but her body wouldn't obey her.

"Me too," she whispered.

They lay in silence. Summer fought the urge to close her eyes, battling against the unconsciousness that threatened to engulf her.

"I really thought we would find him," muttered Jonah, so softly she could only just hear him.

"Me too."

Mount Necros was silent. The children lay unmoving on the mirrored mountaintop. Their quest for home, their quest to find the king, was in tatters.

Summer gazed up at the mirrored shards, letting the shifting reflections at the corner of her vision remind her of their time in the kingdom. The friends they had lost, and the darkness and brokenness of this beautiful world.

There were so many images. Hundreds, thousands of pictures that flickered past, almost too quickly to see. Some were familiar, others strange and unknown, but all showing a kingdom that was dying: chaos, disease, destruction, and pollution.

Her heart ached to find the king. They had come this far – they mustn't fail. Even if she could not move, while there was a single breath in her body, she had to keep trying.

"King!" she croaked as loudly as she could, realizing for the first time she didn't even know his name.

"King!" She tried louder, her dry throat hurting with the effort.

"King!" she called with every ounce of her desperation and frustration.

"King!" She heard Jonah's cracked voice join her cry.

"KING!" they shouted together, loud enough for the word to echo between the mirrors.

Summer tried to call again, but her voice failed her; nothing but a croak coming out. Beside her, Jonah lapsed into coughing.

The echo died away.

Summer let her heavy eyelids droop. Each blink lasted longer as opening her eyes became more difficult. The mountaintop blurred, the shifting reflections faded.

One shape – like a single person – remained consistent amidst the shifting pictures. It grew larger, coming toward them, weaving its way between the mirror shards. Summer blinked hard, willing her eyes to clear. The shape was a man, dressed in dark rags. His face was blurry and indistinct. He moved purposefully toward them, stopping directly over their limp bodies.

The man gazed down at them for a long while. From the corner of her eye, Summer saw Jonah's hand loosen its grip on the crown he had clung to since Ellenair's fall. He was too weak to push it more than a few centimetres along the dusty ground, but his intention was clear.

The man stooped, touching the crown lightly.

A tremendous crash of thunder shook the mountain. The brooding sky boiled into a whirlpool of darkness as a wind stronger than a hurricane whipped it into a twisting spiral. The images in the mirrors bloomed into vividness, suddenly clear and distinct.

Thousands of glimmering shards reflected Presadia in all its pain and chaos. In each mirror, the sky swirled, just as on the mountain. Summer saw forests, where the howling wind tore the blackened leaves and dead branches from the trees. In one mirror, the dwarfish treasury was melting, gold and silver pooling on the ground and dripping into deep cracks in the earth. In another, the wooden throne in the Silver Wood was eaten by worms, and in yet another, she could see Khoree's great body, half buried in the mountainside, lifeless and alone.

Sad images, terrible images, of things she had seen and parts of

Presadia she knew nothing of. It was an endless barrage of reflections. There for a moment, gone the next. Each one of a kingdom dying.

She could see the howling hurricane ripping through the kingdom, causing havoc and destruction in its wake and pulling the evil fog up into the growing tempest.

So much. Too much. Summer couldn't comprehend the scale of the storm. Couldn't bear the heartache of the pictures of brokenness that kept coming.

Summer closed her eyes in the knowledge she wouldn't open them again.

The tempest swirled ever more powerfully around Mount Necros, forming a cyclone of choking black. The mountain's crown of mirrors blazed like the sun. The tornado spun faster and faster, the tail plummeting toward the ground, toward the two unconscious figures; toward the man.

It struck him like a spear. With a cry he threw open his arms, as if to embrace the cloud of darkness that spiralled down into his fragile body. There was a crack like thunder and the earth itself shook. And still he stood.

The intensity grew, the shrieking tornado sucking up the earth and stones and swirling them all in a display of awesome raw power.

Then, with a sudden thrum of silence, the last of the tornado was absorbed into the man. He remained standing a moment more, before crumpling to his knees and falling to lie beside Summer and Jonah.

On the mountainside, all was silent.

The sky, hidden by cloud and fog for so long, was now a clear blue. The last rays of the evening sun refracted and reflected in the prisms, bathing the mountaintop in a golden light. A thousand rainbows caressed the three figures that lay motionless and broken on the dusty floor.

Two children, filthy and small, and a broken man in shabby clothes, unremarkable but for the four-stranded crown he wore on his head.

26

THE KING

Jonah blinked.

He turned his head to shield his eyes from the brightness of the midday sun. He lay where they had fallen. His body still ached, but it was no longer the agony of total exhaustion; more like a healthy ache – the kind you get the day after you've done something really active. He could smell something wonderful, a warm comforting smell. Wood-smoke, and something baking.

Cautiously, he rolled over, waiting for his battered body to protest, but he felt surprisingly good.

Summer was lying nearby. Her eyes were closed, but she looked peaceful, and the gentle rise and fall of her breathing reassured him.

Fighting the desire to wake her, he looked around him instead.

They were still on Mount Necros. Now the sun was shining, the crystal crown on the mountain peak was dazzling with brightness and beauty. The sky was clear with only the faintest hint of haziness on the distant horizon. It was a natural bluey colour, far different from the unnatural yellow smog that had choked the land previously.

Between Jonah and that far-off point was the whole of Presadia stretched out below him, as it had been when they flew over with Khoree. Now, for the first time, he saw it as it was meant to be. Breathtaking. Great forests, and rivers of brilliant blue; mountain ranges – inconsequential in comparison to Mount Necros, but majestic nonetheless – divided fertile valleys, like the ridged spines of dragons. In the far distance, he could see an azure ocean.

Myriad reflections bounced from the mirror shards, but the midday sun made the glass shine so brightly, it hurt Jonah's eyes to look.

Closer to them, a person was hunched over a small fire. His clothes were tattered. Jonah would have taken him for a tramp if it hadn't been for the fact he was wearing Ellenair's crown on his head. He was baking what looked like flatbread over the coals, using a mirror shard to poke the embers.

As if he sensed Jonah staring at him, the man raised his head.

"Jonah, good morning. Or, I should probably say, *afternoon*. Are you hungry?"

He was hungry. Famished, in fact. And thirsty too. He wasn't sure how the man knew his name, but the smell of the cooking quickly distracted him from the question.

The man gestured for Jonah to join him at the fire.

"I have plenty. Come and eat. You have earned it!"

"Who are you? And how do you know my name?" asked Jonah, his eyes flitting back to the crown.

"Do you not know who I am?" the man asked.

"You're…" Jonah hesitated, hardly able to believe what he was seeing. "You're the king?"

The man smiled.

"As for how I know your name, I have been watching my kingdom through the mirror shards, including your journey here."

Jonah wasn't sure how he felt about that. He stretched, looking at the shards in their dizzying shift of half-pictures and vivid colours. The smell of the bread was too alluring though, and he joined the king at the fire.

The king gave Jonah some of the fresh bread. It was just cool enough to eat, and delightfully warm and crisp. For Jonah, who hadn't eaten properly in days, it was the best thing he had ever tasted. The man passed him a leather flask filled with water, fresh and deliciously cool.

"You came a long way to find me, and it cost you a huge amount, but you persevered. You showed more courage than you ever believed you had, and you helped turn others from the wrong path. Because of that, you have helped restore the land to how it was always meant to be."

"We have? How?"

"Our actions don't just affect ourselves. They impact others. In small ways, our actions affect the entire world. All the things you have done might seem inconsequential, but they have helped transform Presadia, helped bring it back to how it should be."

Jonah felt confused, exhilarated, and peaceful all at the same time. They had done it.

"I had started to think we would never find you. I didn't think we could get here."

"Even small steps in the right direction add up, you know. Before you realize it, you're halfway there."

"Jonah?" Summer sat up and stared around her in wonder. "We're alive!"

"Summer! Look, it's the king! We actually found him!" He thought to himself for a moment and added, "Or maybe he found us."

Summer stared at the man with the crown. Jonah could see the same doubts in her eyes as he had felt. The king looked unremarkable and ordinary, only the crown setting him apart. For Jonah, the doubts were fast fading though. There was something about the man that instilled confidence in Jonah. The crown didn't look out of place despite his beggar's rags; instead, it seemed to complete him. Jonah helped drag Summer to her feet and pulled her closer to the fire, offering her the bread and water. She drank great gulps of the water and eagerly accepted the bread.

"We didn't see you arrive," she said to the king. "What happened?"

"Something that had to happen," he replied. "Something I knew must happen long ago. It was the right time."

"For what?" asked Summer.

"A long time ago I lived in this kingdom and I ruled its people. The land was fair and all was well, but some thought they could do a better job without me. They tried to overthrow me and seize my power for themselves. They threw me out of Presadia and turned their backs on me." His face was sad as he recounted the tale. "They fought and made a mess of the kingdom. They took what they wanted without caring how it affected others, and they forgot about me. Some denied I ever existed!"

"Didn't any of them stand by you?" said Summer.

The man's mouth lifted in a small smile. "Yes. Some did. Some stayed loyal to me, trusted I would come back and make things right again. They made mistakes too, but they tried to do the right thing, even when I was not there with them. They believed I was still alive, and that one day I would wear this crown again."

"I'm... I'm glad you got it. Ellenair..." – a pang of grief made Jonah stumble over the words – "she wanted us to give it to you."

"When you put it on..." Summer hesitated, remembering what she had seen in that terrible moment, "everything went dark and stormy and... and then I don't remember."

"Yes. It had to be dealt with." The man looked solemn. "A good king takes responsibility for his kingdom. He is exalted in its triumphs and shamed by its failures, even when those failures are not of his own doing. Putting on the crown again, all the mess and trouble that has happened since I last wore it was my responsibility once more."

"But if it wasn't your fault...?" put in Jonah, confused.

The king chuckled.

"Yes, you're right. It's easier to be responsible only for yourself, for your own actions, and thoughts, and words. But in answer to your question, Jonah, I did it for one reason only, and that was my love for this place and for these people.

"You probably think kings look down on their people; all high and mighty and concerned only with passing judgments and handing out punishments, that kind of thing. But a good king isn't like that. A good king loves his people as if they were his children, and he wants to look after them and give them the best. Sometimes that means dispensing justice, but often it means sorting out problems that were caused by someone else. A good king puts his kingdom and its people before his own happiness, and he would do anything for them. For a good king, no cost is too high."

Jonah thought about that for a moment. It brought to his mind their long, hard journey and what it had cost the friends they had lost in the gruelling climb up Mount Necros.

He felt the king's eyes on him. As though he knew what Jonah was thinking, he said, "You're remembering your friends?"

Jonah nodded. "How did you know?"

"The mirror shards show much to those who know how to use them. It is why I came here. I may not have sat on the throne for a long time, but that doesn't mean I have not been watching over my people." He paused, his lips quirking into a smile. "Come. I have something to show you."

He stood and walked away from the fire and down the gentle slope, where the mirror shards were smaller.

They approached a small ridge from where they could see the whole kingdom spread out, like a living map, below them. The slopes and cliffs of Mount Necros dropped away beneath the ridge, plunging down for miles. Jonah was amazed to think how high they had climbed.

After they had stood there for several silent minutes, surveying the scene, Summer asked, "What are we looking–"

Her question was interrupted by a distant sound. At first, Jonah thought it might be the hoot of some strange bird, but a moment later it resolved into a whooping cry.

Jonah frowned, scanning the mountainside for the source of the noise.

Without warning, a huge shape burst out of a deep ravine further down the mountain.

27

THE NEW KINGDOM

"Khoree!" Summer squealed in delight. "She's alive! How?" The explosion of happiness in Summer's heart was almost too much to contain.

The dragon's mighty wings beat their way higher and higher. Her scales had been blue before, but now they shone like a jewelled ocean. She roared with joy as she saw them, the sound cracking like thunder and echoing around the mountainside. Twisting her huge body with the gracefulness of a swallow, she performed a somersault in the air, and the two passengers holding tightly to her scales became visible.

"It's Tin! And Ellenair!" Jonah danced with excitement. "They're all here! How?"

The king didn't reply, instead only laughing with joy at the spectacle. Summer found she didn't mind. So many of the questions that had been burning within her felt somehow less important now she was here. Instead she allowed the uncontainable sense of delight and joy to blossom within her.

The whooping sound appeared to be coming from Tin, who was having a whale of a time. Even Ellenair was smiling. She looked much as she had done when they first met her, but now her beauty seemed to radiate like the sun. Her elfish skin had taken on some of the dragon's vibrancy, which contrasted with her intricate tattoos. The overall impression was truly striking and like nothing Summer had seen before. She sat straight-backed and regal on the dragon as if she were on a prize horse, yet her posture had none of the arrogance or pride she had once shown.

As Khoree came closer, Summer could see there was something different about Tin's appearance. His beard was no longer sad and stubbly, but once again long and thick. It was not the silver it had been, but a resplendent gold and woven into plaits.

The mighty dragon landed with surprising nimbleness close to them. Looking up at the king, Summer saw he was beaming with pride and love.

"Friends," he called to them. "Welcome! And well done!"

Tin and Ellenair dismounted, sliding down the curve of Khoree's wing to reach the ground.

Tin, as boisterous as he had always been, ran to the king and dropped to one knee.

"Mighty king, it is an honour to be in your presence. I can barely believe it! The dwarfs of Val-Chasar are your committed servants. I…" Tin's confident voice choked. "I am sorry, your majesty, for the way the dwarfs have lived… the way *I* have lived. We let our greed rule us. We claimed to be loyal to you, but I fear our actions showed a different story. Perhaps my efforts have earned me some forgiveness for our past mistakes?" He lifted his eyes pleadingly to the king.

"It is not by actions that you earn forgiveness, High Lord Tin," said the king, and a flash of concern crossed the poor dwarf's face. "True forgiveness is only possible when you come to the realization that you need to be forgiven. Actions are important, but they are the fruit of what grows in your heart. What you did to help these two you did for me." His voice softened. "You do not need to earn my forgiveness; I give it freely." He leaned down and raised the dwarf by his elbow. "Arise, dwarf. I accept your allegiance, and the loyalty of the dwarfs of Val-Chasar."

Tin stood up, his face flushed with happiness.

"And what about you, old friend?" The king turned to Khoree. The dragon shuffled awkwardly, hanging her head like a guilty dog.

"Come, Khoree – don't stay back there. Come close."

"It has been many years, my king," mumbled Khoree, as much as a dragon could mumble.

The king nodded. "But not even dragons live long enough for it to be too long to come back to me. I have longed for you to return. I have missed you dearly and it is very good to see you."

Khoree lumbered nearer, bowing her long neck low to bring her head close to the king.

"My dear Khoree, you were blessed with as many years as you could ever desire, yet you chose to give that up to get these two here."

"They are special to me," Khoree told him. "They showed me I was flying in the wrong direction and helped lead me back."

She turned to look at the children as she spoke the words. Summer felt a rush of love for the irritable old dragon who had done so much for them. She reached up to hug her thick neck.

The king looked on, smiling.

"You truly are the wisest dragon ever to live. Your wisdom may look strange to this world – to give up immortality for a pair of children – but it is the truest wisdom anyone will find."

Khoree bowed her head, her face glowing, and reptilian eyes shimmering with what could only be tears.

"And as for you, Ellenair..."

Before he could say anything else, Ellenair let out a strangled sob and crumpled in tears at the king's feet. Her loss of composure startled them all. It was only then Summer remembered Khoree telling her how Ellenair had once been pledged to marry the king.

Now the distraught elf queen wouldn't even raise her face to look at him.

"Your majesty! I am so sorry. So, *so* sorry. I had given up hope of ever seeing you again. But here you are! I tried to remain faithful to you when you left. I tried to make things right, I tried to keep order and control. Even when we retreated to the Silver Wood, I thought I might be able to make things right. Years went by and you didn't come back, and by that time, everything was a mess. I still thought I could fix it for you before you returned. I just wanted to rule as well as you did. I thought I could. I tried, but–"

"Hush, Ellenair," the king said softly.

"Please! I know you will probably never want to see me again, but let me at least remain near you. I'll be a servant. I never meant to get so caught up in ruling; it just kind of happened. It took a dragon kidnapping me to make me realize how selfish and proud I had become."

"Ellenair." The king said her name again softly.

"*Please* forgive me. From now on, no one shall call me queen. I should never have called myself that! I could never be your queen now." She wept bitterly at his feet.

The king crouched down. Stretching out his hand, he lifted her chin to look her in the eyes.

"Ellenair, my treasure. The past is forgotten."

She nodded, her face wet with tears. "Of course it is, my lord. I know we could no longer be married, not after everything I have done."

"That is not what I meant," the king replied patiently. "I forgive you completely, you must know that. I see before me someone worthier than ever to be queen of this kingdom. Humility is the most important quality for a king or queen. We shall be married, if you still wish it, and I will rule with you by my side."

Ellenair wept again, but this time with tears of joy.

Summer blinked back tears of her own as the king raised his bride to her feet. As he kissed her, Jonah pulled a squeamish face and Summer burst out laughing.

The king looked at them both and smiled.

"This kingdom owes you a great debt. You have been here such a short time, but your actions have brought change everywhere you have gone. You have reminded people of what is important, and you have made this moment possible. How may I reward you? Ask, and it will be done."

Summer looked up into the king's kind eyes.

"All we want is to get home. The mirror that brought us here was destroyed and we don't know how to get back."

The king chuckled. "That, dear Summer, is easily done. The mirror of which you speak was made from the crystals found here on this mountain. If you know how, they can open a doorway to any place. I have used them often over the years I have been here. People had rejected my kingship, but I could not abandon Presadia entirely. Perhaps I could not work in the same way as when I sat on the throne, but I did not desert my people. Those who turned against me had to deal with the consequences of those actions; had to see the troubles that their attempts to take control or make themselves rich had in the long run. Much wrong has been done in Presadia and the land bore the marks of that wickedness. I have wept often watching the suffering that has taken place. I have visited and been with my people in the difficulties, just another homeless peasant in beggar's rags. But with a quiet word here, a nudge there, I have still been there in the tough times. I love this kingdom too much to ignore its pain, but I had to wait. I had to wait until people turned to me again and recognized the need for my kingship. The mirrors allowed me to visit all the corners of Presadia whenever I pleased, but I knew that one day Presadia would find its way back to me."

"But Presadia isn't our home," Summer explained.

"I know. But your world is only another reflection of this one. It is more alike than you might think. The mirror shards can take you there also."

"But we don't have to go straight away, do we?" piped up Jonah beside her. "I wouldn't mind seeing more of Presadia. I'm not sure I want to go back yet. Things here are so much more exciting and magical."

Summer thought back over the last few days and wondered if "exciting" was the word she would have chosen. But then, looking at her friends, and the king, and the hundred thousand reflections of the beauty of Presadia, she realized how attractive Jonah's suggestion was.

"This place may seem more exciting and magical to you," Khoree rumbled, "but that's only because it's not *your* world. You get used to your life and stop realizing how exciting your own world is. But there will be adventures waiting for you there. Quests that need to be completed. Perhaps it is not so different from being here after all."

"He is right, you know," chirped Tin. "You have done much here. Personally, I am more thankful to you both than I could ever say, but there will be people in your world who need your help as well."

Ellenair nodded. She was once again composed, and smiling now. "If I have learned anything over the last few days, it is that sometimes we have to abandon our own desires to play our part in the bigger picture."

Summer looked at them all. The thought of leaving was deeply sad, but their words were wise and true. She turned to Jonah.

"I think they're right. Our parents must be worried sick about us, and we are only visitors here. We always said we just needed to get home. You never know, maybe we can come back again someday?"

She looked at the king hopefully.

"Maybe you can," he agreed. "You are always welcome in my kingdom, just as I hope I would be welcome in your world."

"Of course you would!" Jonah assured him earnestly.

"I fear not all would agree. But maybe by what you do and say, you can prepare a way for me. But now, what is your decision? I can open up a doorway here and now."

Summer nodded. Something she could not explain told her they had completed their purpose in this place. It was time to return home.

The king walked to the nearest mirror shards.

He rested his hand on the shifting surface of one of the shards, the images blossoming into clarity at his touch.

Summer drank in the pictures of the kingdom, trying to remember every detail. The pictures showed a kingdom put right, broken things restored. Many of the pictures showed people, of all races, gathering together in excitement, or in some cases trepidation. The miraculous transformation of Presadia was apparent to anyone. Summer didn't know if the people knew it had been the king, but they certainly knew something big had happened. She wondered how they would react when the king went down from Mount Necros.

Gradually, the flickering images slowed, finally halting on the image of a dark room. Summer could just make out the bell ropes of the church tower in the gloom.

"The way home," the king said simply.

"I'll miss you all," Summer said, looking around at their companions.

"Me too," said Jonah.

"And we you," said Khoree. "You helped us see what we could be. Never has anyone so young and so small transformed me as much as you two have."

Tin slapped Jonah on the shoulder and gave Summer a tight squeeze. "You may not have any beards, but if you ever return, you will be the guests of honour at Val-Chasar."

"Travel well, Summer and Jonah," said Ellenair, grasping their hands in turn. "Remember the lessons you have learned here. Live them out in your world. Persevere as you did here. It has been a privilege to meet you both."

Summer gazed at her friends, unable to find words to convey what she was feeling. Jonah too seemed at a loss as to what to say.

"Goodbye," he said finally.

Summer clasped Jonah's hand, and the two of them stepped into the mirror shard.

CHAPTER DISCUSSION QUESTIONS

If you want to chat with others about what happens in the book, why not discuss some of the following questions. These are great for a book club or class, or to use as a family.

1. THE SECRET PASSAGE

Jonah is proud of how fast he can run. What things do you do really well? Where do you think the tunnel will take them?

2. TRUE REFLECTIONS

The writing on the mirror asks, "Face yourself, what do you see?" Is it easy to face up to ourselves? What do you think you would have seen in the mirror? What sort of person would you want to become?

3. GONE

When Jonah realizes Summer is gone, he is panicked and anxious – but also brave. Have you ever been in a situation where something has gone wrong? How did you react?

4. THE PRINCESS

Summer ends up telling a lie and pretending to be a princess. Do you think this was the right thing to do?

5. ESCAPE

After following Summer through the mirror, Jonah bravely sets out to find her. How do you think he was feeling? Do you think Jonah is a good friend?

6. THE LONG-LOST KING

Tin described the sad state of the kingdom. How do you think Presadia ended up like this?

7. THE SCAVENGERS

The dwarfs were making the villagers work for next to nothing. Do you think this was fair? Are there things in our world that seem to treat or use people unfairly that you know of?

8. VAL-CHASAR

Antimony stands out from the other dwarfs. Why do you think this might be? Why do you think the other dwarfs don't treat him differently?

9. THE DWARF LORD

The dwarfs treated Summer and Jonah very differently. Why do you think they did this? Do you think it was the right thing to have done?

10. THE DWARF'S DEEDS

What do you think the verse of the poem meant when it said, "Beliefs are dead when missing deeds"? Do you think the dwarfs were living out their beliefs and words? What do you think about Tin's reaction?

11. KHOREE'S LAIR

Jonah upset the dragon with something he said. Have you ever experienced a time where something that was said hurt you or someone else? Do you think Khoree was right to get so angry so quickly?

12. A DRAGON'S RIDDLE

Khoree's riddle said, "I am small, but I steer the whole." How do you think the tongue does this? Do you think you can "tame" your tongue? Can you control everything you say, or do you sometimes say things you regret?

13. THE DRAGON'S SECRET

Khoree let her mistakes of the past hold her back. Have you ever stopped yourself doing something because of a previous mistake or bad experience? Do you think you could try again now?

14. THE TONGUE-TAMER

Tin and the dwarfs made the "tongue-tamer" to help cool Khoree's tongue and her fiery temper. Have you ever had friends help you out with a problem? What helps you to "cool down" when you get angry?

15. THE SILVER WOOD

The elves were able to heal the sickness in the trees and care for nature. Do you think it's important to look after the world around us? What things can you do to try and help our own environment?

16. THE ELFISH QUEEN

Summer bravely spoke up, even though she must have felt very nervous. Have you ever had to speak up even when it's scary? What do you think about the welcome given by the elf queen to the children and their friends?

17. KIDNAP

Why do you think Ellenair was reluctant to help them? What would change for the elf queen if the king did come back?

18. THE QUEST TO FIND THE KING

What sorts of things did you notice as they flew over the kingdom? Why do you think it's important that the children and their friends find the king?

19. MOUNT NECROS

The flying was difficult for Khoree due to the nasty clouds. Why do you think she kept going?

20. KHOREE'S BREATH

Khoree was willing to give anything for their quest. What most stood out to you in this chapter? How did her sacrifice make you feel? How would the other characters have felt?

21. THE CHASM

Did you expect Ellenair to keep going with the others? Why do you think they all kept pressing on despite how hard the journey was? How must they all have felt when they reached the chasm?

22. THE DWARF'S TREASURE

Tin's beard was what entitled him to all his wealth and his position as high lord of the dwarfs. Why do you think he cut it off? Have you ever given up something really special for someone or something else? Is it easy to give something up that you care about?

23. THE CROWNLESS QUEEN

Ellenair says, "I have clung to this crown my whole life... I didn't want to surrender my power." How much has Ellenair changed from when the children first met her? What do you think caused that change?

24. MIRROR MOUNTAIN

Jonah and Summer's journey becomes extremely difficult and unpleasant. What strikes you about their perseverance? How do you think they kept going? Have you ever struggled to keep going and "finish it"?

25. PRESADIA FALLEN

What do you think about when the book says, "… while there was a single breath in her body, she had to keep trying"? What do you think happened when the man took the crown? Who did you think the man was?

26. THE KING

Is the king like you expected? What do you think about the king's words: "Our actions don't just affect ourselves. They impact others. In small ways, our actions affect the entire world"? Do you think that's true? What do you think about what the king did for his kingdom?

27. THE NEW KINGDOM

Were you surprised to see the others again? How did it make you feel? What did you think about each of the characters meeting the king? How do you think Summer and Jonah changed after their adventure in Presadia? Do you think they would do anything differently when they returned home? Do you think you have changed at all from reading the story?

The Mirror and the Mountain
and James

It's possible to link the story to the book of James in the Bible. The different verses of the poem relate to five main threads in James's five chapters.

Face it: In the first part of the story the children have to "face it"; looking into the mirror to see what they are truly like (warts and all) as well as how they could be. In chapter 1 of James, the author uses an image of a mirror in relation to the Bible. It's through looking into the Bible that we learn to see ourselves completely honestly and as God sees us. Since none of us are perfect, it reveals to us what's not good: the places we have messed up and the damage we have done to ourselves, to others, to our world, and to God. But it also shows us an insight into the people God has truly made us to be. James tells us that looking into a mirror but then forgetting our reflection is a waste of time. Likewise, when we look into the Bible and face up to the reflection we see, we must allow it to shape and transform us. When we pay careful attention to the picture of ourselves that we see when we read the Bible, we have made the first important step towards becoming who we truly can be.

To link the book with this lesson from James, why not spend some time discussing the scenes in which Jonah and particularly Summer "face it" by seeing their reflections in the mirror? If used in a group setting, you could organize a quiet reflection where children draw themselves in a print-out of a mirror frame and write or think about how they think believe God sees them.

Live it: James 2 is famous for its controversy around the discussion of faith and works. Some have at times believed James to promote a works-based approach to faith where we earn our salvation through what we do, rather than through faith in what God has done. This is a misreading of James's teaching, however. The book of James, chapter 2 in particular, is pointing out the hypocrisy of claiming to believe one thing but seeing no evidence or reflection of that in what you say or do. What we do is not the most important thing; rather, what we do reveals what we believe. James explains this well when he writes: "Suppose a brother or a sister is without clothes and daily food. If one of you says to them, 'Go in peace; keep warm and well fed,' but does nothing about their physical needs, what good is it? In the same way, faith by itself, if it is not accompanied by action, is dead" (James 2:15–17). In *The Mirror and the Mountain,* this hypocrisy is illustrated through the dwarfs. They claim and believe themselves to be faithful followers of the king, but their actions go directly against his practices and principles. The favouritism they show to Summer over Jonah is much the same as their exploitation of the poor villagers.

When linking the story with the book of James, the theme of "live it" is a great chance to look at social injustice or exploitation. Our own society is uncomfortably close to that of the dwarfs in this regard, with the unfair trade practices, sweatshops, and modern-day slavery that underpins a consumeristic society. A project could be identifying and finding out information about organizations like Fairtrade Foundation. Another simple activity could be creating two sets of cards: beliefs and actions. Mix them up and get the children to try matching the pairs.

Tame it: James 3 dedicates a large section to "taming the tongue". Words are undeniably powerful. They can build up or tear down. By our words we often shape the direction of our lives. Khoree's struggles with her own tongue illustrate the way in which sometimes our tongues can seem to control us rather than the other way around. Khoree also embodies a larger lesson around "tame it", however, with her words connecting to an explosive temper. Taming it is about controlling ourselves, whether our words, tempers, unhealthy or excessive appetites, or anything else that has a hold on us. Watching what we say is a valuable lesson to explore with any children, but for some, reflecting on how to tame anger might be particularly important.

A great activity to do with a group would be to have an ice cube and a glass of warm water. Drop the ice cube into the glass. While the ice is melting, get them to think in their heads about times they have spoken unkindly or become angry. When the ice cube has melted, brainstorm some ideas together for how to tame our tongues and control our anger.

Lose it: A hallmark of the Christian faith is sacrifice, most clearly exemplified in Jesus' own sacrifice for us. We see particular examples of sacrifice from Khoree, Tin, and Ellenair on the mountain. Although sad, these show the reality and difficulty of sacrifice. If it were easy, it wouldn't be sacrifice. Sacrifice comes from a place of humility, through viewing something else as more important and worthy than what you are giving up. James 4 picks up on words from Proverbs, used by Jesus in his own ministry: "God opposes the proud but shows favour to the humble" (James 4:6). Ellenair stands as perhaps the clearest example of a change from pride to humility in the book. Using her as the basis for discussion would be a great way to link to James 4.

A practical application could be to get children to think of something they have, maybe some sweets or a favourite toy or possession, that a friend or a sibling would like. Challenge the children to be sacrificial with what they have and to share with or give it to someone else.

Finish it: James 5 addresses patience in suffering. Perseverance is a key theme of being a Christian and a common thread throughout the book of James. In the story, the journey up Mount Necros takes everything the children have. It's a truly terrible and difficult journey, but the key to perseverance in the Christian faith is that there is hope. Not a vague wishy-washy hope, but a promise that Jesus makes all things right in the end. In the words of the Bible: "...be patient and stand firm, because the Lord's coming is near" (James 5:8). In *The Mirror and the Mountain,* the characters are driven by their hope and faith that the king will make all things right in the end. The mountaintop scene is an imperfect image of Jesus' costly kingship through which he takes on responsibility for the whole of his kingdom, fixing all that was broken and awakening his followers from death to life.

A great activity would be to write some things that are ongoing struggles for the children, or for the family, that require perseverance. Keep these somewhere convenient and set a reminder to get them out each day, or once a week, and keep praying for them. Over time, talk about how you have seen God answering those prayers (maybe in ways you didn't expect).